To Byzantium

ILLINOIS SHORT FICTION

Other titles in the series:
Rolling All the Time by James Ballard
Love in the Winter by Daniel Curley
Crossings by Stephen Minot
A Season for Unnatural Causes by Philip F. O'Connor
Small Moments by Nancy Huddleston Packer
Curving Road by John Stewart
Such Waltzing Was Not Easy by Gordon Weaver

To Byzantium

Stories by
Andrew Fetler

UNIVERSITY OF ILLINOIS PRESS

Urbana   *Chicago*   *London*

© 1962, 1966, 1967, 1968, 1969, 1970, 1971,
    1972, 1976, by Andrew Fetler
Manufactured in the United States of America

These stories appeared originally, in somewhat
different form, as follows:

"To Byzantium," *New American Review.*

"The Mandolin," *Malahat Review.*

"The Mozart Lover," *Northwest Review.*

"Longface," *The Atlantic Monthly.*

"Afternoon of a Sleepwalker," *Epoch.*

"The Pillow from Niagara Falls," *Antioch Review.*

"In Line for Lemonade," *Malahat Review,* included
    in *Short Stories from the Literary Magazine,* ed.
    Jarvis Thurston and Curt Johnson (Glenview).

"Demons of Nikolai," *Kenyon Review.*

"Shadows on the Water," *American Review.*

Library of Congress Cataloging in Publication Data

Fetler, Andrew.
    To Byzantium.

        CONTENTS: To Byzantium.—The pillow from Niagara
Falls.—The mandolin.—The Mozart lover. [etc.]
        I. Title.
PZ4.F42To [PS3556.E84]   813'.5'4   76-13854
ISBN 0-252-00583-X
ISBN 0-252-00584-8 pbk.

For Carol and Jonathan

Contents

1 To Byzantium

15 The Pillow from Niagara Falls

27 The Mandolin

32 The Mozart Lover

52 Demons

69 Longface

78 In Line for Lemonade

86 Afternoon of a Sleepwalker

92 Shadows on the Water

To Byzantium

Among my brother's effects in the cardboard box I brought home from the hospital at Newhall, California, was a photo of my mother—her last formal portrait at 71—and, stuck in the frame, a snapshot of himself. The snapshot shows him standing on the steps of our church in the Los Feliz hills overlooking Los Angeles. Feet apart, arms folded over his chest, head high in half profile. So he had treasured this snapshot. I had taken it eight years ago, the day after we buried our father. My brother had marked an X in the gravel before the church, the spot where I was to stand with his camera, and I had watched him through the viewfinder as he struck his pose and gave me the word to snap the picture.

He loved being photographed, to record important moments in his life. I had taken pictures of him in the graveyard, where he had stood meditating at our father's grave. And next morning he got the flash attachment and had me photograph him sitting at our father's desk, pen in hand and an expression of deep thought on his face. After lunch he dragged me out again, and there we were, before our father's church.

"That's wrong," he said, before I could snap the picture. "I should be facing the door." He faced the church door and struck his pose again, head high and arms folded. "How's this?"

"Great."

"Are you getting the cross on the door?"

I hadn't noticed. "I'm getting it," I said. "Are you ready?"

He drew a deep breath and pushed out his chest. "Go ahead."

The doctor at Newhall said my brother had swallowed enough pills to kill a horse.

He never showed me this picture, and now that I have it I feel mildly surprised at seeing the resemblance between my father and my brother. In life, the only resemblance I saw was that between the real thing and a distorted copy. In my mind I had never admitted my brother to my father's company.

But I had not known my father when he was as young as my brother. In my earliest family album is a yellowed snapshot of my father on those same church steps in 1932, when he broke with his American patriarch. Except for his beard and priestly robes, he looks like my brother's double—feet pugnaciously apart, the points of his shoes sticking out from under the hem of his cassock, head high in half profile, and arms folded inappropriately over the cross on his chest, as if he had forgotten this burden hanging by a chain from his neck. The same stance of defiance as my brother's, the same self-conscious air of nobility and Old World earnestness and innocence of irony. Father and son.

My father was one of those rare émigrés who came out intact one step ahead of the Revolution. With nobody but God to guide him, he sank his entire inheritance into the church and the hillside it stood on, which he christened Old Russia, only to see his inspiration frowned upon by his new ecclesiastical superiors, whom he had thought to surprise and delight with his monument to Holy Russia.

What the difficulty was, exactly, I don't know. Unlike my brother, I could never appreciate theological niceties. I suspect that my father's quarrel with his superiors in 1932 was less a matter of theology than taste. These beardless American priests with their cars and radios could be expected to look doubtfully at a church that seemed made of Christmas cookies and peppermint sticks, and wonder at its builder. His eventual excommunication, which he lived to regret, made him no less Orthodox in his own eyes. He revived liturgical variants heard since the seventeenth century only in the Monastery of the Grottoes in Kiev. He dedicated an arbor in our garden to the memory of an ancient abbot, and hung an image of St.

Vladimir in the church beside the Holy Mother of Kazan.

I have a funny friend in Boston, an Irishman, who bangs the table with his fist when he talks, and having yelled himself out asks with a timid smile, "Isn't it?" or, "Am I not right?" He likes to hear about Old Russia. His father was a boozing Irish Catholic, a Boston patriot who bounced through the streets on a fat beer horse, at the head of his precinct on the Fourth. And although his father's memory embarrasses him, he will arise and go to Galway and Galway Bay, and parade through town with hat and cane and two fine setters in leash, some day. Yet his irreligion is loud and emphatic. When he talks about religion he seems to be talking about sexual repression, and his voice loses the resonance I hear in his Irish jokes.

His example cautions me. As a child I must have been exposed to a good deal of resonance. I had an edifying hallucination, for example. I saw the great Los Angeles fire when I was twelve, which engulfed the houses and temples and plazas from Hollywood to Santa Monica. I stood by the gates of our Old Russia in the Los Feliz hills, between the Swiss chalet and the Taj on adjoining hills, and watched the smoke roiling over the rooftops far below. The merchandise of gold and silver, and precious stones, and of pearls, and fine linen, and purple, and silk, and scarlet, and all thyine wood, and all manner vessels of ivory, and all manner vessels of most precious wood, and of brass, and iron, and marble, and cinnamon, and odors, and ointments, and wine, and oil, and fine flour, and wheat, and beasts, and sheep, and horses, and bodies, and souls of men—all up in smoke in that city, wherein were made rich all that had ships in the sea by reason of her costliness. My father's incantations at the table lulled me to sleep in those days. I may have seen a movie of a city burning. I asked my brother, my senior by seven years, and of course Los Angeles had enjoyed no such conflagration. But I know the revulsion Los Angeles arouses in travelers. One fine morning those miles of glitter will be gone and the desert stretch to the horizon where the city had stood.

Our own forty acres of poplars and silver birches, like the Taj on the next hill, were rented to film companies. Nothing was native to the place—neither plants nor people, nor religion. My father built

Old Russia because he could not go back to his century. We did not
read Soviet writers there, but the old romantics. You left your car by
the wooden gates and walked up an avenue of poplars to the priest's
house. I must have been thirteen or fourteen when I realized that we
had become professional ethnics. You might see my parents slouch-
ing in rattan chairs on the veranda, the samovar steaming between
them. My brother would be playing old liturgical music on the upright in the parlor within, cluttering the music with expansive orna-
ments all his own, trills and gorgeous arabesques, giving expression
to his sense of well-being and delusions.

There would be a reason for my brother's musical inventions. He
was tormented by the imperatives of moral purity in the morning,
crushing boredom and drowsiness at noon, and lust at night. He had
a passion for logic and could spot inconsistencies, and picked fights,
interrogated, quarreled. I don't know if he ever changed anybody's
mind, but he claimed victories in the meeting halls he frequented in
his exhausting search for God and women, among the sects and
societies that litter California's coast. He could not sin deliberately,
with a will, but only on the sly, behind his own back. Then he confessed his sins to his own heart, damned himself, and read poetry
about the night of the soul. In this manner he purified himself, and
at the piano added grace notes in transports of redeemed innocence.

I sat on the couch doing my homework. He played the piano with
his head thrown back and eyes closed. Communing. A strong scent
of lilac drifted in through the open window. Then the vacuum cleaner began to whine upstairs, and the music stopped. Above the noise
of the vacuum cleaner we could hear our mother singing to herself.

"What is she doing?" he said, glaring at the ceiling.

"She's vacuuming your bedroom."

He turned on the piano stool. Whenever he bothered to look at me
I had to brace myself for some challenge or other. "Why," he said,
folding his arms, "are you sitting there? I'm really interested."

"I'm doing my homework," I said piously.

"What homework?"

"Math, if you must know."

"What will you do with math? What will you measure? This

house? I mean, how is it with people like you? Do you ever stop to think *why* you do anything? Or do you just do your homework, as you say?"

"I don't know," I said, to irritate him, and gave him my stupid look.

"Fascinating. You eat, you sleep, you run about like a dog. Doesn't it hurt you to live like a dog?"

At that moment our mother appeared on the stairs with a red kerchief on her head and a rag in her hand. "Did you throw a razor blade in the sink?" she asked him.

"That's all right," he said. "It's used up."

My father, too, found it painful to live with one foot on earth. Nothing consoled him for his expulsion from Russia, and in the wild hills above Los Angeles he fought off barbaric America to preserve a quality, a tone, a style. In his defiant days he had built Old Russia to the glory of God with materials scarcely more convincing than those of Disneyland. Old Russia transported him to Byzantium. He could not turn from that dream, and sought to restore his losses with plaster and paint.

Our wooden church walls were made to look like stone three feet thick, but they housed a real church. My father was an actor, yet a priest. The rituals were charades, yet redemptive. Everything was faked except the corpses in our graveyard behind the church. The corpses were real. The years had decimated Old Russia. The resourceful in my father's congregation, the born criminals, caught on to insurance in Toledo, Ohio, or the stock market in Chicago. The old were dumped by their children in commercial nursing homes. A nervous poet who used to walk our paths with a book under his arm tried Mexico and cut his wrists. "In this life to die is nothing new—but to live, of course, is not new, either." And the second-generation children roared up the hill in blue and red sports cars of a Sunday morning, to see the religious antics their folks had been up to a million years ago. When they slammed out to the beaches, the dust they kicked up drifted in the sun past the veranda with its rattan chairs and samovar stand.

Two old babas lived forever, it seemed. Long black skirts, white kerchiefs, chattering up the path, taking Easter cakes to the church. Inside, they kissed the stone floor which I was supposed to have mopped. Down on all fours like two wolves, pressing their mouths to the stone, drinking the spirit. They kissed holy pictures, walls under pictures, each other, and my father's hand when he approached in his priestly robes. He suffered them, and loved them, but sought refuge at the altar, turning his back on the thirty unbelievers who had been herded in from the heat outside from a sightseeing bus parked by the gates.

Small-town librarians and schoolteachers, in respectful attitudes, hands folded, their faces stiff and reserved, noses sniffing the incense in the artificial darkness, eyes staring at the flame before the Holy Mother, and feet edging toward a wall or pillar as the service dragged on. He refused to install chairs or even benches, as in the valley the Greek Orthodox had done, and would not cut a minute of his interminable ritual. Two sightseeing companies in Hollywood struck him from their itineraries, and Pleasure Tours complained they were stopping too long between the Taj and Homes of the Stars. But the priest worked the altar as if God's clemency depended upon it. The church choir had long since disappeared, to be replaced by my brother at the organ in the balcony, where he played his responses to my father's exclamations at the altar, yanked the rope that rang the bell, and squinted down at girls like a prisoner from his cage.

We rotted on that hillside as if cut off from the Body of Christ, not serving but catering, tourists having replaced believers. From time to time, when threatened by bankruptcy, we sold bits and pieces of Old Russia to subdividers. Pretentious houses crawled up the hillside, with billboards advertising "Paradise Now!" and "Heavenly View!" The sick old man, cornered by Los Angeles, clutched his stomach with one hand and dragged himself up and down our paths, around the church, to the graveyard and back, lashed by the far din of the construction gangs.

No continuing city. He grew small and bent, and forgot to comb his beard, but remembered to greet my mother in the kitchen, on the morning of Easter Sunday: "Christ is risen!" And she answered,

"Verily, He is risen!" He delayed going to church as long as possible, cooling his tea in the saucer and playing with a vest button hanging by a thread. I sat watching him. A boy of fifteen can hurt to see his priest and emperor reduced to a caterer.

"Dad?" I said. "Why do the tourists have to come on Easter Sunday?"

"Don't bother him now," my mother said. "Go find your brother. It's time we started for church."

"I can't tell them to go away," my father said to her.

"Of course not."

"Jesus died for them, too. What would He think of me?" And he gave me an astonished look.

From the gates the Pleasure Tours bus honked twice to announce its arrival, on Easter Sunday as on any morning, starting him to his feet. Then my brother, twenty-two at the time, whom I once caught in the vestry trying on our father's priestly robes, stuck his head in at the door and yelled, "We're late!"—and ran.

My father hobbled out the back way. I followed him the length of our garden and out over a turnstile beyond the church grounds proper, the long way around, past construction lumber and foundation pits gouged in the hillside, over land no longer ours, to avoid visitors with cameras. In the old days he used to like being photographed. No more. Now, he stole into the vestry by the back door, and we did not speak as I attended him and he dressed for the show that was not a show. He took the amethyst from the jewel box I held for him, and put it on his finger. He took the chain and kissed the cross and hung it round his neck. When he was ready, when it was time to show himself to the people, he turned instead to the mirror beside the alcove.

I saw an expression of curiosity flickering in his eyes. In the balcony my brother had started the music for his cue, but here the priest stood, absorbed by his image in the dark glass, seeming not to know himself, forgetting his vocation. Then he caught my eye in the mirror. "After all is said and done—" he began, but did not finish. We stood looking at each other, father and son, and when his cue came and went and he did not move, I knew something awful was happening.

Priest, father, emperor in his splendid robes, he stood looking at
me with a petrified expression in his eyes. His lip gave a twitch, and
all at once he sank to one knee and embraced me. Pulled me into his
arms and held. My confusion cut loose from my lungs a derisive
laugh, and he leaned away, his body wobbling on one knee as if I had
plunged a dagger into his chest. He screwed up one eye, giving me an
uncomprehending look.

"Tell them to go away, Dad. Please? Tell them to go *away!*"

Then he understood, and he wrung my name from his throat as if
I had been weeping all along, all along. I fled. I ran the length of Old
Russia in the fragrant morning, and hiding in a pile of lumber heard
the bell strike, and burst into tears.

We never drew so close again. At fifteen I did not know how, and
he denied himself his last vanity—a son's love.

About that time my brother discovered his mission: to stop the
religious freak show in Old Russia and turn the church to a true
worship of the Divine Spirit. My brother felt more comfortable with
the Divine Spirit than with God and Jesus Christ. But he could not
speak of such reforms to our father, and bided his time running after
girls in the I-Thou Temple in Hollywood.

He sat on the veranda after dinner, reading the paper and burp-
ing. He had always been too old to play with me, absorbed in matters
too elevated for my understanding, but he liked to instruct. If I
wanted to sit with him, I had to be instructed.

"Where's Dad?" he said, as I sat down beside him.

"In his room."

My brother put down the paper. "He doesn't know what he's talking about. He's never been to the I-Thou Temple. It's not at all like
the Church of the Open Door. At the I-Thou it's all interpersonal.
Do you know what that means?"

"No."

"That means your fellow man is not an It, he's a Thou. If you treat
a person as a thing—as Dad treats me, for example—you only iso-
late yourself. We call it alienation. That's what Dad suffers from—
alienation. He's finished."

It would have seemed so, at first glance. From my brother too the old man averted his face. He subsided and sank from us, deaf to us, locked up in himself. One thing remained for him to do, to unburden himself of a last burden, without debate, without seeking my mother's counsel. Clutching his stomach, he had my brother drive him down the hill to the District Court to have his name changed from Viliki to Krotki. To the judge who granted his prayer neither name meant anything. Viliki means great, and Krotki means gentle. I could not make a fuss about the new name devolving upon me as a minor. With a different breakfast in his stomach, my father might have chosen a name like Unknown, or Clean Spit. But my brother stormed, wanting his father's true name. And he kept his father's true name, having attained his majority when our father humbled himself.

I went away to college, and to war. And when I came home from the war, when I myself felt like a tourist in Old Russia, I saw my father sitting in his rattan chair on the veranda. He blinked his watery eyes at me and pulled from his pocket a caramel coated with dust and a curling white hair. "For your sweet tooth." He had the quiet insanity of a well-behaved child. He made a joke about his new name which he repeated at odd moments at the table, diverting him more than us. "Yes, it's true," he would say, apropos of nothing. "I went out great, and the Lord has brought me home again gentle."

In my mind I have a heaven for him, and a chair to sit in, by reason of that same disastrous Sunday morning, when after all was said and done he wished to abide if he could in Jesus Christ, that he might have confidence and not be ashamed before Him at His coming.

So he died. And my brother felt born again. He played with his father's jewels, wore his father's tattered bathrobe, slammed doors, and ignored the dinner bell as his father had ignored it before him.

Having heard the icy call of the Lord, my brother assumed that he was chosen. He believed every spirit that came to plead with him from every corner of his possessed soul. My brother the inheritor stretched his arms as if waking from a long sleep, yawned, smiled, spat. Alive to himself, not doubting himself, not puzzling himself.

And went out to look at Old Russia, to see what all needed to be done, and had me photograph him on the church steps for a historical record, his feet apart and arms folded over his chest, not having been shot dead to himself by the Implacable Hunter.

He still ran after girls at the I-Thou Temple in Hollywood, and came home to argue that nothing could revive Old Russia except an ecumenical spirit. He spent an afternoon framing a photo of our mother for his nightstand. "We have a date Saturday, you and I," he joked with her.

No joke. He took her out to rich dinners she could not eat and movies that put her to sleep. He brought her home exhausted and confused, and at midnight shook her from her snooze in her rocker, and dragged her to his bedroom for prayers, to pray with him as she had prayed with our father. "Yes, yes," she would say, staring about at the charts and religious posters and mystical symbols on his walls. "Yes, dearest, let us pray. God will forgive everything." He kept her on her knees for thirty minutes, as he read from some greasy pamphlet or other, and sent her to bed with a reminder that they had a date Saturday. Then he sulked for days and ignored her, and prayed and fasted alone by her photo in his bedroom.

In our climate every conceivable religious plant creeps, slithers, entwines, snaps, exhales, twists, breeds in the sun. My brother felt at home in this jungle. He knew what to do and how to go about it. Not to repeat his father's mistakes, he did not have himself ordained, but took care to be licensed by the I-Thou Temple. He sat at his father's desk, stuffing his head with catalogs of metaphysical distinctions and occult fads. Late at night he pored over geometric figures, circles detached and overlapping, and triangles with an eye at the apex, and crosses formed by the asymptotes of hyperbolas, and psychospiritual organizational tables that would have impressed General Motors, and calendars of duties, and charts tracing his personal oscillations through the darkness and the light. During my visits, I might have learned something about him if he had expressed a preference for chocolate ice cream over vanilla. But he had become a Deep Thinker and was not accessible.

When next I visited, a small billboard had been erected over the gates. "Welcome To The I-Thou Russian Church." The parent Temple in Hollywood encouraged him to keep what he liked of the old rituals and wardrobe. For two years our scandalized Orthodox remnant probed the thickets of a lawsuit against my brother, and settled out of court for the best slice of the land, where they proposed building a modern Orthodox church with indirect lighting. Old Russia was reduced to the priest's house, the church, and the grave-yard.

"How I pray he marries!" my mother said to me in the kitchen, cutting away the rot from potatoes. She had grown old and had begun to forget English and sometimes sprinkled sugar on her stew. "You must know some good girls. Can't you take him away from here, to meet your friends?"

"My friends are trivial. He's too deep for them."

"Why are you nasty? You know nothing about him."

"Don't you care what he did to the church?" I asked.

"Did what! Now we have a fire insurance! If it burns down we can build again."

My brother never found the wife he thought he wanted, the young girl his fancy installed at the organ in the church balcony while he celebrated the I-Thou mysteries at the altar. The balcony spot went to a paid organist from a Fundamentalist radio station that advertised professional anti-Communists, itinerant faith-healers, and blest handkerchiefs. With the help of this musicologist he put together a service from the more dramatic parts of the Orthodox ritual and Fundamentalist clatter. The tourist clientele fell off, the Orthodox ceased altogether, but varieties of existentialists got wind of the new thing in Old Russia and flocked up the hill.

His success should not have astonished me, I realize now. He was a compulsive talker, loved to preach, and during a Latin collect he moved our father's Bible from the gospel side of the altar to the epistle side without rhyme or reason. In the vestry after the service he asked me to help him with his robes. "How was I?" I had never seen him so elated. He offered me the job of sacristan—room, board, and pocket money. Well, how was he? When you stripped his sermon of fashionable words like *existential* and *ambience*, and mystical pre-

tensions, and a love of spectacle, you saw a simple commitment to
the old verities. Seeing him there in our father's priestly robes, pulling in the new breed of celebrants who lounged about in comfortable
Balaban & Katz chairs—"No Smoking!"—I thought the church felt
as secure from disintegration as it had felt in the old days, before
Pleasure Tours and subdividers had sniffed its carcass.

Tea on the veranda as in the old days, and the lilac bloomed. My
brother ran into the house to fetch his Plato, and came out turning
the pages of the book nearsightedly, impatient to enlighten my dark
mind with Plato's delightful passage about the heavenly pattern. He
coupled his rhetorical questions with other questions and other
premises, breeding monsters of logic with several heads and tails,
but I understood him to mean that we lived in a finite universe, and
the earth stood fixed at the center of the spheres of sun and moon,
the stars and all the planets. He did not say these antiquated things,
but with the lilac's thick fragrance in the air he made me feel them,
and I thought him beautiful as he read, holding the book close to his
nose: " 'In heaven,' I replied, 'there is laid up a pattern of it, me-
thinks, which he who desires may behold, and beholding, may set his
own house in order. But whether such a one exists, or ever will exist
in fact, is no matter; for he will live after the manner of that city,
having nothing to do with any other.' "

"That's good," I said.

"How can you say that's good," my brother cried, "and not
believe? If you don't believe, then you are not moved. If you are
moved, then you must believe."

"All right, I believe."

"But you don't! Why are you lying?"

In those last days, before my mother's death and my brother's commitment to the hospital at Newhall, if you happened to come by on a
quiet afternoon, left your car by the white gates and walked up the
avenue of poplars to the priest's house, you might have seen the old
woman sweeping the veranda, and heard the piano tinkling in the
dark house within. She would have been anxious to please you, and
might have taken it into her head to show you the church. Descend-

ing sideways down the steps, favoring her stiff leg, she would have approached you with her hands clasped in an expression of pleasure. A new face!

What part of Russia did you come from? Had you known her husband? *This way, this way!* she would gesture, her English fading. She might tug at your sleeve and step back to have a better look at you, working her gums, smiling and pointing to the church. Did you come to see the church? You would look into the trees where she pointed and see something golden and white behind the green foliage. *So nice, so nice!* she would seem to say, laughing soundlessly, and start up the path. *That's right, come along, I'll show you everything!* You would follow past neglected flowerbeds and unpruned bushes, past a dilapidated arbor and a rain-warped orange crate standing in the high grass and nettles. At a turn in the path by a dead lemon tree she would suddenly stop and stretch her neck forward like a buzzard, to see if the church was still there. Yes, her old eyes could see it still, and she would give you a look of infinite gaiety. Could you see it? Could you see what she saw?

You might, if you happened to be in Plato's mood.

If not, you would see that the church in Old Russia was not a bad tourist stop, as such attractions go, the blue doors and windows decorated like Christmas cookies, the pillars twisted into candy sticks, and the large golden onion at the top sprinkled with blue stars. This dome, you would see, pleased the artist enough to add two small domes as an afterthought, asymmetrically, one near the main door and the other half sunk behind the vestry gable. Something to photograph, if you photograph such things.

But if you did not calculate the uses of such a place and were in no hurry to see the Taj, if for once you were neither rich nor poor, felt neither trapped nor abandoned by life, and sensed a momentary order in your soul, you might have stopped beside the old woman and stood still with a small intake of breath, and heard the wind in the grass and seen the church floating in the sky.

The old woman who had blossomed there, and was soon to die like her lemon tree, would not trouble her mad son for the keys. Giving the church door a shake to show that it was really locked, she would pull you round to a smaller path grown over with weeds, where the thick bushes darkened the earth and the damp air would chill your feet.

This way, this way!—and you would follow her to the very spot where Emil Richter filmed the closing scene for his *Fathers and Sons*. The willow he planted grows aslant the stagnant pond to this day, hanging its unkempt head over rockweed, skunk cabbage, pond scums, stoneworts. As you approached you might hear the plash of a toad, and lifting your eyes see the luminous algae glowing darkly with emanations from the dead. Mr. Richter was fond of a melancholy little bench, where Bazarov's old father sat watching as his wife touched up their son's grave. For years that bench lay overturned in the grass behind the compost heap, but when my father died my mother dragged the bench to his grave.

"My husband," she would tell you, smiling gaily and inviting you to sit and look at death. "Did you know him?"

The Pillow from Niagara Falls

During his four years in Iowa City, Steve Calvin had spoken to Joe Dilko only twice: once, when Dilko handed out free bread rolls from a shopping bag in Bernie's Bar, the second time when he came round to the Young Republicans with an offer to read his zoology paper, "Ion Regulation in the Isolated Hind-gut of the Cockroach, *Byrsotria fumigata*." You could not tell whether the farm boy was crazy or putting on. Since Dilko did not picket for Civil Rights, or paint, or sing at hootenannies, nobody could figure out why his gyroscope had broken down. When he dropped out of school, items about him began to appear in the *Register*. He was stopping at farm houses in the southern counties, scaring folks with his beard and rags as he came from the cornfields to ask for something to eat. He was on his home ground, then. Sheriffs chased him out of their counties and he drifted north. Folks debated what to do about him when he disappeared. A friend of Steve's heard that Dilko had sailed to Europe.

Three years later, on a trip to Chicago for his father, Steve Calvin saw Dilko on Erie Street off Michigan Avenue, warming his hands at a fire in an oil drum before a wrecked mansion. The old garden wall had been knocked down and from the muddy garden the wreckers had dragged to the rubbish heap the statue of a monk.

After a moment's hesitation, Steve crossed over. The street was wet, and in the stinging wind Dilko wore a dirty sport jacket over a sweatshirt, baggy corduroy pants, and torn sneakers without socks.

Steve introduced himself. "You wouldn't remember me," he apologized, looking at the red eyes in the hairy, wolfish face. "I was one of the Young Republicans."

"Oh, ya."

"I heard you'd gone to Europe?"

"Ya."

"We went last summer. Rome, mostly."

Shivering, Dilko glanced at Steve's attaché case, kid gloves, hat, and turned back to the fire in the oil drum.

"What's this monk?" Steve asked, not wanting to let go.

"They're fixing to melt him down to a washing machine."

Steve looked at the statue. A nice monk, he could see, with a big nose and a fat belly under that cassock. The head was turned to one side, as at a sudden alarm, and from the broken hand hung rusted wires.

"I wouldn't mind having it," Steve said.

"It's worthless. Bastards used to import this junk from Italy, for their hog yards."

They could have done worse, Steve thought. The closest thing to religion at home was Sound Fiscal Policy. Nobody would ever raise a statue to Reverend Otis Peavy. Benson, Iowa, had no sculptor, and Otis Peavy did not deserve one. Neither did Dad, for all he had done for the town. When folks died in Benson, they were buried in the ground and forgotten, like his mother.

"How about having dinner with me?" Steve said.

"You paying?"

He had meant to dine at Fritzel's, where he might see someone from Lerner & Gipps. He took Dilko to the Corner House, where the walls were hung with framed photographs of accordion artists, tap dancers, song stylists. In the warm light of the restaurant Dilko's face bristled with hairs and his eyes looked inflamed. He wanted the specialty of the house, fried chicken, drank Scotch, and started his second drink before the herring was served.

Steve Calvin had little to say about his honeymoon in Rome, and his partnership in his father's sheet-metal works did not interest Dilko. Calvin & Son was not big by city standards. They employed

104 men, not counting office help, and made parts for electric cranes, dummy torpedoes for the Navy, grenade containers, "U.S." mail boxes. There was a dairy in Benson, a bottling company, and two lumber yards, but none of these amounted to much. What kept the town going was Calvin & Son. As Steve talked, Dilko was slopping up the herring.

Not very interesting, Steve realized, and shut up about himself.

"Don't you like Benson?" Dilko asked hoarsely.

"I hate it."

"What do you want? Chicago?"

"I can't leave the business. It's in the family."

"That's funny," Dilko said. "I want to go back to Iowa."

He had been in Chicago only a month, having returned from Greece, expelled by the new Athenian policy against penniless Americans. All the same, he had learned something. If you put plumbing before dancing and singing, you are an ape.

When the chicken was served, he grabbed the breast and tore it with his long yellow teeth.

Steve could imagine him dancing and singing. He said, "What were you doing in Greece?"

"You know where Atana is?"

Sounded like a small town in Iowa or Illinois. "No," Steve said.

"Do you know *anything* about Atana?"

Steve couldn't say he did.

"It's down from Piraeus. No electric lights. No washing machines."

The old church at Atana stands high on a barren hill, with a view of the sea. Evenings, Joe Dilko sat on the cemetery wall and watched the Greek men dancing the Greek dance. Had Steve ever seen the shadow that moves before a flame over a sheet of paper, as it turns black? That was how you could see the night coming over the sea when the men danced the ancient dance under the turning constellations.

Steve put down his fork, listening.

"I can't do the Greek," Dilko said. He made to snap his greasy fingers. "See that? I'm not Greek. I'm Zebedee, Iowa."

Sounded drearier than Benson. "What's in Zebedee?"

"Fifteen hundred hardshell Baptists."

Dilko took a gulp of water, rinsed his mouth, swallowed, and fell to gnawing his chicken again. Steve sat watching him.

"You got folks in Zebedee, Joe?"

"My mother. All dog except her brain. That's part dog, part human."

"Is that why you want to go back? For your mother?"

"Not my mother." His shaggy head hung over the plate as he spat out bits of skin and talked. "She's got this pillow she bought in Niagara Falls when she got married. Work of art."

Had Steve ever seen the painted novelty pillows with green tassels?

"You're going back for a pillow?" Steve asked him.

"Ya. I want to see it again."

He wanted to see all of Iowa, in fact. He would wander around in Iowa as he had wandered in Greece, and try to find some value he could call his own. If you don't have your own culture, you have nothing. You are a tourist in Atana. In Iowa, Joe Dilko was not a tourist, no more than his mother was. You saw her type throughout the Midwest—long neck, low forehead, small eyes—her stiff mouth unsuited for forming words. Yet this same woman kept an altar to the graceful powers that make men good, and by sheer instinct wrought a symmetry as deep as Plato's. For on the upright piano in the parlor, under a print of a Caucasian female she thought represented Jesus, she propped the pillow from Niagara Falls between cut-glass lamps on fluted doilies, which she laundered, starched, and ironed in April and October. The pillow showed Niagara Falls, shrubs and rocks in the foreground and a sunset sky in the background, all painted in luminous yellows, greens, pinks, and asbestos white. "To look at, not touch!"

So Joe Dilko was fitting himself out for his return to Iowa, for tramping the roads and towns of Iowa, to see what he could see. The suit he needed cost seventy dollars at Army Surplus: all of one piece, waterproof, felt lining. When you zipped yourself in, you could sleep in a ditch snug as a rabbit. It had zipper pockets front and back.

"You're the only rich bastard I know," he said. "You don't have

to give me the money. Just buy me this suit. It's the only good thing
Calvin & Son will ever do."

Steve Calvin did not buy him the suit, but he gave him ten dollars.
The dirty hand turned the bill as if it were a piece of wilted lettuce.
When he was gone, Steve smoked a cigarette, looking at the torn
chicken on Dilko's plate. The skin hung over the edge of the plate,
and the bones lay scattered on the table. He asked the waiter to clear
away the mess and ordered another Scotch.

His own mother had not owned a pillow from Niagara Falls. Her
treasures were more expensive, choking the attic of the old house in
Benson where Dad had lived alone since Steve and Holly moved into
their new colonial on the hill south of town. Steve would have liked
to throw gasoline on his mother's things in that attic and light a
match. In the last year of her life she was taken by a madness for
mail-order buying. With her husband away at the plant and her son
in college, she would sit alone in the dark parlor, reading women's
magazines. God knows, maybe she remembered the friends she had
not corresponded with since her high school days thirty years before.
She cut out the coupons, stabbed the letters with her small pinched
hand, "Mrs. Henry Calvin," and sent them off to get something
from the mailman. China dolls, Navajo rugs, Masterpieces of the
Ages, New England antiques, British woolens, genuine Mexican pot-
tery. In the end, the pain in her tortured body crashed through the
drugs and she fell into her coma gasping amid all that rubbish.

His father, old Henry Calvin, never talked about her death, and
nobody in Benson ever asked. At the funeral in church, Peavy said
from the pulpit that Jesus had taken her to a better mansion. Then
they had driven the corpse to the cemetery at fifty miles an hour and
were back in twenty minutes. Henry Calvin's grained Midwestern
face showed no emotion. But from time to time, especially on festive
occasions, he broke into violent fun resembling grief. He might have
a cry first, as he did in the Cow Palace in San Francisco at the 1964
Republican convention, when the choir sang "Mine eyes have seen
the glory" at a ripping quick-march, the voices hard and clipped like
singing commercials. A Goldwater hat on his head, Henry Calvin
stamped his feet, blew a paper trumpet, and climbed on his chair,

yelling along with the crowd to drown out Governor Rockefeller's protesting speech. "What did I tell ya!" he said to his son, his face flushed
with drink and heat, at the height of the noise. "We got 'im!" Steve
held him by his jacket to keep him from falling off the chair as the roar
against Rockefeller crashed over the acres of faces. A man behind
them yelled, "We're running this show! We're running this show!"
You could get drunk on that alone, the sense of power that went even
to Steve's head, rocked by the mad laughter of a winning team. Dad
had loved everybody in the hotel lobby in San Francisco. Peering
about with bloodshot eyes, swinging his arms, he hugged a small man
with a pasty face, a member of the Washington lobby against import-
ing Japanese wire. Following them into the bar, Steve got slaps on the
back from drunk Nebraska rednecks with cowboy hats. On the televi-
sion screen, in the tobacco smoke, Richard Nixon was neatly adjusting his tie. Dad bought the Nebraskans drinks and showed them his
son, Steve Calvin of Calvin & Son. They had all made it to San Francisco, by God, and old Henry Calvin drank standing at the bar with a
foot on the brass rail, as if he had escaped from his wife's death on the
prairie to lawlessness in the West.

What did Joe Dilko see in his mother's pillow and things like that?
Steve's own mother had left an attic full of things like that, and all of
Benson was nothing but things like that. No, he would never have
gone back to Iowa if it hadn't been for the business, which was in the
family.

But Joe Dilko came back for nothing, as it seemed to Steve Calvin,
in the summer following their dinner in Chicago. He tramped the
county roads as before, and the *Register's* stringers used him good-
naturedly for fillers. "Dilko Rides Again." Picked up for vagrancy in
his own county, he was given ten days in jail for resisting arrest and
disturbing the peace. More often, sheriffs took him to the county line,
sometimes giving him a dollar to keep moving. "Dilko: There Is No
California." He was described wearing army fatigues and an Air
Force jacket. A Legion post protested to the *Register*. He was also
blamed for strayed cats, open pasture gates, one barn-burning, and
the theft of gasoline from farm pumps, though he traveled on foot.
When the weather turned cold in the fall and it became apparent that

Joe Dilko meant to tramp right on through the winter, folks in Benson said that he ought to be put away for his own good.

Sometimes in his bed at night Steve Calvin's eyes opened on the dark ceiling as he heard, far away, the wail of the night train on the prairie. To Council Bluffs, where the old wagon trains used to line up for the West. He got the shakes, then, for no reason he knew, and pulled Holly into his arms. "What is it?" He couldn't tell, except that he wanted to get away from Benson.

He and Dad had planned a last day of fishing before dry-docking the boat for the winter. At four o'clock of a Saturday morning in October, Holly sat in the lamplight at her dresser, combing her hair. Steve liked to look at his wife. He had seen such girls on the ski slopes in Aspen, their faces pretty and healthy. 4-H had done it, the prettiest, healthiest thing America had produced, exciting his lust. Holly was the type that could catch a ball and bake her own bread. In Iowa City, she had helped to picket a beauty parlor that would not serve Black coeds.

"Your cereal's ready," she said.

He had to dress and drive through the town to the jetty on Cranberry Lake.

"Dad's probably still in bed," he said, padding up in his pajamas.

"Dad's probably waiting for you on the boat right now."

"I want to," he said, his hands on her neck.

She put down the comb. His mouth was on her ear and his hands on the cord of her robe.

"I've been waiting to tell you," she said. "We're going to have a baby."

"Since when?"

"I saw Dr. Williams Tuesday."

He pulled on his woolens for the long cold day, his old fishing pants, boots.

"It doesn't have to change anything, does it?" she said, sitting stiffly before her mirror.

"It's not the baby. I just don't want to raise my kid in Benson."

He followed her into the kitchen, which, with its curved service counter, sliding panels, dishwasher, freezer, electric range with buttons and clocks, was a marvel of time-study design, a dietician's laboratory. He sat on his bench in the breakfast nook.

"Is Dr. Williams sure?"

"Would you still love me, with the baby?"

"It's not the baby."

"I don't want the baby to make a difference."

"It won't."

She sat down on his knees. "We can go anywhere you like, can't we? I'll get out your old knapsack and you can grow a beard, like Joe Dilko."

He sat holding her on his knees, smelling her perfume. "Sure, I'll grow a beard. They'll think I'm a Commie."

As he piled his fishing gear into the jeep, she came out to him with the picnic basket for the boat. It would be a fine day, he saw. The stars were out. Beyond the lake, the light of the grain elevator at Four Corners glowed on the horizon.

"I'll anchor off Willow Point," he said, zipping his jacket.

"Kiss me."

He kissed her. Then he kissed her again.

"You're glad, aren't you, Steve?"

"I told you, it's not the baby. I hate this goddamn town."

Hoarfrost glistened on the road in the headlights as he drove to town. Jefferson Street was deserted under the streetlamps, but as he turned the jeep into Madison Street he saw Dad's Cadillac with three other cars, and a light in the sheriff's office. Four men stood on the pavement by the cars. Behind them the dark courthouse, an old pile of stone, resembled a bulging carpetbag some giant had dropped on the prairie in his flight to the West.

"What's up, Red?"

Red Martin, a shotgun in the crook of his arm, broke from the men. "That Dilko guy. Sheriff wants to bring him in."

Steve got out and nodded to the Jones brothers, both holding shotguns and wearing hunting caps, and young Walter Setchell in his Legion uniform, who had set off firecrackers in the Palladium last Halloween. Men from the plant, locals born and bred—high cheekbones, large ears, small eyes slanted in the night. Ferrets. They stood watching him, smoking cigarettes.

"Dilko bother anyone?"

"Stole a chicken from Ben Yost. He's somewheres around Four Corners."

As Steve mounted the steps to the courthouse, Sheriff Torpey came out, followed by Dad with his white yachting cap on his head.

"You knew Dilko in college, Steve?" Torpey asked.

"Sort of."

"He ever carry a knife or a gun?"

"No," Steve said. "You got the guns."

Torpey gave old Henry Calvin a look, and said, "We don't get out there, Ben will find him and blow his brains out."

"I'll pay for his goddamn chicken. Dad, tell 'em to lay off. Dilko may be hungry, sometimes, but he's not a thief."

"They found the chicken at Sid Fey's," Torpey said.

Steve had hunted pheasant around Sid Fey's, the shack of a recluse, dead and gone. "I'll pay the damages, Mr. Torpey."

"What they *didn't* find was any signs of a cooking fire. He must have swallowed that chicken raw."

Henry Calvin said, "Leon figured you might talk to him, if he doesn't want to come in."

"We don't have to talk to him, Henry. We aim to find him and cool him off."

A handsome man of sixty, tall and strong, Torpey walked down to the men with the casual, somewhat weary manner of John Wayne. Resting on one leg, hip out, he spoke to them. They scattered to their cars. The two Jones cars had no mufflers. Standing on the pavement beside his father, Steve saw them leaping to the chase, their engines exploding. They had the street to themselves in the dark before dawn, and permission to hunt a man with a beard. The Jones cars roared off as in a drag race—a black-and-yellow Chevy with red trim, and a red Pontiac with a yellow stripe down its back. Torpey followed in his car like an anxious parent. The posse would have to split up at Four Corners, Steve realized. The Jones boys might spot Dilko in some field far from town, where none might see. The street stood silent and empty again, the lamps shining on the dark store fronts.

"You been funny ever since you come back from school," Henry
Calvin said to his son. "All right, that's all right. But now you're fun-
ny when it's a shame to you and to me, insulting Leon to his face.
How can you do that to me, boy?"

"They'll kill him."

"You could show some respect for the law in this county!"

Henry Calvin drove his Cadillac, switching on the radio. Cowboy
voices howled a gospel song to the accompaniment of electric guitars. Beside him, sunk in the soft upholstery, his son watched the
road. Out of town, their headlights picked up a tilted Royal Crown
Cola sign on the prairie, then a Jesus Saves, then two abandoned
farm houses, their unpainted boards weathered black. Left to rot.
Dilko's mother's pillow, he thought, and things like that. He glanced
at his father's face in the soft green light of the dashboard. Had this
ugly country never bothered him? Had he never hated himself?

As they drove by Sid Fey's shack, Henry Calvin said, "That's
where Dilko ate that chicken."

Steve sat up in the warm Cadillac and peered out into the night.
On the horizon, dawn was breaking.

"This friend of yours," Henry Calvin said. "What did they throw
him out of college for?"

"He wasn't thrown out. He quit."

"What's he want in a dump like Four Corners?"

"Maybe he figured it wasn't a dump."

He must have been crazy. He had limped six cross-country miles
before he found a barn outside Colby and hanged himself. The cold
sun had cleared the horizon as they pulled up behind a line of five
cars and two pickups. In the yard stood a state patrol car and a white
ambulance from Hoover Memorial. The farmers had seen the body
in the barn; they loitered in the yard to swap news, relaxed and
friendly. Henry Calvin joined Sheriff Torpey and the Jones brothers,
who had left their shotguns in their cars. Steve went to the barn.

Someone had dragged the body to the threshold and thrown a
horse blanket over it. The feet stuck out. What he could see of
Dilko's famous Air Force uniform was torn fatigues. Sneakers without socks. The ankles were scratched, and the right ankle was swol-

len and blue. He seemed smaller than Steve remembered him in Chicago. A bit of cloth, a pair of shoes.

"It's all our fault," Henry Calvin said as they drove home. "He should have been put away a year ago."

Steve wanted to stop at Sid Fey's shack.

"What for?"

"I want to see."

He wanted to see what Joe Dilko had seen.

Henry Calvin turned off the radio—he couldn't stand the thing when not driving, and couldn't drive without it—and settled back with a cigar. Steve got out and walked up the dirt road to the shack. Over the door, he saw, Sid Fey had nailed a horseshoe. His forty acres had long since reverted to the bank and gone to weeds. Good pheasant country.

He pushed open the door with his foot. Through the cracked roof, sunlight shivered the gloom within. He looked around, breathing the dank smell of decay. The walls still held, patched with burlap and tar paper, Sid Fey's last effort. Dilko may have guessed yesterday, as Steve guessed now, that Sid Fey had swept the room from time to time, and tidied his cot. Scattered about the floor were beer cans, whiskey bottles, and flattened cigarette butts, flung there by resting hunters. In the sink, under the rusted hand pump, lay the chicken in a pool of blood, its belly torn open, its feathers stained dark.

He went out and stood in the yard, breathing the air. In Dilko's place, where would he have gone from here with a sprained ankle? He looked north, studying the land. South? Both prospects terrified. An ocean of lights and shadows on the prairie.

"What you see?"

"The chicken's there, all right."

"It's not seven, yet. You still want to go fishing?"

"I'd rather go home, Dad."

"Sorry. I didn't think you knew him that good."

Both fell silent. Henry Calvin drove slowly into town. Steve looked at the houses as if he had never seen them before. It was as if he could see, through Dilko, something worth looking at in Benson, after all. Jefferson Street was still deserted. The green awning over

Campbell's Shoes flapped in the early sun like an abandoned tent. Sam's Diner had disappeared some years before. It used to stand between Western Auto and Lavinia's Beauty Shoppe, having started as a covered wagon in Cowboy Calvin's day. Now, grass had sprung up in the space Sam had occupied. All of Benson had once been a camp of covered wagons. If you drove slowly down Jefferson Street on an October morning, you could see where the covered wagons had stood in the tall grass. You could almost hear the small toneless voices singing on the camp grounds, as nowadays they sang in Peavy's church: "Oh, who will come and go with me? I'm bound for the Promised Land." Folks in this way station to the Promised Land had been singing the song for a long time now, generation after generation. That many had grown weary and lain down to rest, to travel no more, had never been officially acknowledged. The map of Benson in the phone directory identified every public building and park except the cemetery, which faced the West.

"Dad, we're going to have a baby."

Henry Calvin said nothing, listening to the cheap cheerful morning music on the radio as he drove. He pulled up by his son's jeep before the courthouse.

"Why don't you come over for dinner tonight?" Steve said, and noticed that the old man's cheek was wet. The radio played and his hands held the wheel.

"Fine," Henry Calvin said. Then he took his son's hand and held it tightly. "I wish your mother was alive."

Steve stood by his jeep, watching him as he drove off in the Cadillac to his old house. Then the street was empty again. For some moments he remained standing there, trying to see the houses with Dilko's eyes. What had Dilko seen in the pillow from Niagara Falls? As if in answer, Steve had a strange fancy. It seemed to him that Bremmer's was saying to Mayer's Discount, while the other shops crowded near: "We've come far enough, old friend. Let's camp here together." And here they all were, making a circle of hands, the prairie grass lapping at the edges of the town.

The Mandolin

In the railway coach, Natasha and Rodya had a Persian rug in their compartment, a crystal carafe on a mahogany table, two green armchairs, and silk window curtains. At the last moment, when the whistle blew and the wedding guests on the station platform raised a yell, Deniski ran into the compartment with a wild look, gave Natasha his mandolin, and ran out as the train started forward.

Waving good-by, Natasha rested her knee on the upholstery, trying the springs. Outside, behind the crowd, Deniski stood looking at her with an expression of disbelief, so preoccupied with his thoughts that he forgot to wave his handkerchief. Well, what could she have done? Marry Deniski and his mandolin?

When the train had left the city and was crossing the immense wheat fields, Rodya returned from his inspection of the other compartments in the coach.

"There's only one other man here," he said. "Fat."

Rodya had become somebody, Natasha realized, as if she had not grasped this fact when his promotion came. She waited for him to ring for service. What would she order? She was not hungry after the party, and did not want to drink unless he wanted to drink. Perhaps he would ring for the bed to be made?

He noticed the mandolin on the rug beside her. "Deniski?" he asked.

Natasha nodded.

Rodya turned the mandolin over in his hands, tapped the polished wood with his finger, and gave it to her. "It's a good one, isn't it?"

"I think so."

The feasting at the club had been too lavish, he remarked, and for some reason the Secretary had made him feel uncomfortable.

"But why?" Natasha cried. "Everybody loves you!"

"Yes, I suppose."

He did not ring for food or for the bed to be made. He did not even remove his overcoat, and with the hat still on his head sat on the edge of the armchair, frowning at the carpet.

"Darling, what is it?"

"We can't travel like this."

When the train stopped at Kalmyzh, he got out with their suitcases. She followed him, carrying Deniski's mandolin, to a car farther forward. From Kalmyzh they traveled third class, in a dirty car crowded with peasants, bundles, women, infants, garbage, tobacco smoke.

Very well, Natasha thought, coughing and shaking beside him on a wooden bench. Life has begun. We need very little, after all. She looked admiringly at a peasant woman giving suck to her baby. Not vex ourselves with luxuries. A modest house with a view of the Neva, perhaps, and a polished tile oven in the main room.

Impulsively, with a look of pleasure, she turned to Rodya. He sat engrossed in his *Handbook*. He was always working. He never got drunk like Deniski, never sang songs, blushed, or laughed loudly. If he stopped to chat with a friend in the street, he was working.

All right. She would build up his wardrobe gradually, without dragging him from shop to shop. The Secretary had told her of a fine German tailor in Leningrad who had thrashed an apprentice for touching a bolt of cloth with unwashed hands. Then Natasha fancied herself sitting in a blue satin-covered chair at Yakovlev's, examining American socks for Rodya, turning them inside out, stretching them, and ordering ten pairs.

She hugged his arm. "Rodya?"

"What? Where are we?"

Natasha asked how much a small house might cost.

"A house? But I have a room."

"Not now, precious. Later. If we have children."

"What a thing to worry about! How do I know where the Party may send me next? People are thirsting everywhere."

Hours later, when Natasha began to feel drowsy, she begged him to rest his head on her shoulder.

"You sleep," he said. Straining to see in the falling light, he was busy digging up cross-references in his *Handbook*. "I'll wake you if I see something interesting."

She awoke with the thought: We don't know each other. It was night. The train had stopped in a field. At the far end of the car, a small dirty bulb cast a weak light over the sleeping bodies. Outside, she saw no lights, no station, not a house. Rodya held his arm about her, but his arm felt wooden. Although her back muscles ached, she did not stir. Somewhere in the car a baby wailed, and two or three voices quarreled.

She looked at her husband. He was smiling down at her in the dark—unpleasantly. Her mouth had never been so close to his mouth. He had never kissed her. His thin face had an alert, eager expression. Holding her, he sat rigidly, as if petrified, and smiled. Natasha bowed her head, and as her ear rested on his chest she heard the thump-thump of his heart. The train was still standing when she fell asleep again, her back sagging in the stiff crook of his arm.

When she awoke she found herself stretched out on the bench, under Rodya's coat. Her face felt puffed and grimy. In the cold dawn the train was clattering slowly over a bridge. Looking round for Rodya, she saw him standing at the end of the car, talking to a bearded, sallow young man in rags. A common soldier hung between them, evidently drunk, turning his small red eyes from the young man to Rodya and wagging his head.

She waved to Rodya. He saw, but made no sign to her. As she waved a second time, he gave her a look of hate. With lowered eyes she waited for him, and all at once she became aware of the sharp stench in the car, the chill of the morning, the shrill voices of the gabbling peasants, and felt dizzy. She pulled at her suitcase under the bench for something to do, saw his *Handbook* on the floor, brushed the cover with her sleeve, and suddenly slammed the book down on the seat beside her. Then she struggled with the window, and failing to open it sank back and stared at the passing country. In the dirty glass her face hung suspended over the fields turning pale in the dawn.

When at last Natasha looked at him again, he had stopped talking with the ragged young man and now sat alone in the baggage corner, on a wooden barrel, with his back to her. There he sat for two hours, until the train pulled into the small station at Cherkovo. Natasha watched him through the window as he left the car, but lost sight of him in the bustle of peasants carrying baskets of food. From the crowd an old man advanced to her window, holding up a bear rug for her to see, with a bear's head, teeth, and claws. She shook her head, feeling exhausted.

The train was moving again when Rodya came back and sat down beside her. He put something wrapped in newspapers on her lap, and said, "Eat."

With her cold fingers she unwrapped four herrings, a chunk of cheese, two bread rolls, and two apples. Natasha began to cry.

"Eat, eat! We have a long journey before us."

She decided, after all, to eat. Swallowing her tears, she skinned a herring for him as he bit into a bread roll and chewed vigorously. Where did he get his energy? He ate and looked with interest at the passengers in the car. He gazed intently at a man wearing a tall black hat, as if he had some urgent business with him, and abruptly turned his eyes to another face and sought something there. Natasha skinned the second herring for him, then started on her own.

"I have a great deal of work to do," he said.

"Yes, dearest, I know."

"Do you know their misery?"

She had not thought of him, at first, as a young man on the way up. That came later. At first, she had been attracted by his concern for others. He was the most selfless person she had ever met.

"Rodya, why did you marry me?"

"Why?"

He seemed to consider why he had married her, but then dismissed it from his mind. "What I want does not matter. The Party can't use me if I live to gratify myself."

Natasha put down her herring and looked at the dead eyes. She felt a sudden sharp fondness for the smoked creature.

"Listen, my friend," he said. "I am no less an artist than your Deniski. More, in fact. My work needs the most careful balancing of emotions. An inward stillness. You must never interrupt me when I work."

"Did I interrupt?"

"When I was talking to that poor fellow over there."

"I'm sorry."

Look at that forest! she thought, as the train took them through a forest. How could anyone, lost here, find his way again? Life has begun. And she stared at Deniski's mandolin at her feet—poor, shy, incoherent Deniski, who would have been too simple to move from first class to third, if he had amounted to anything. But Deniski did not amount to anything; he would not have been permitted to travel first class. She would have traveled with Deniski third class, as she now traveled with Rodya. Dear me! thought Natasha. Dear me!

The Mozart Lover

Under the green lampshade of Miss Bibo's hallway desk he counted out eighty dollars and the woman gave him a receipt.

"Yes," said the landlady. She turned her pockmarked face away from the lamp. "I prefer romances now that I am no longer young." She spoke with a foreign accent. Hungarian, maybe. Certainly not Czech.

"I would not call you old," Franz said.

"No?" she said, not smiling, and locked the rolltop desk. "Have you been here long, in this country?"

"Two years."

"You know," she said, "I want to go back."

Franz nodded.

"They feel insulted if you want to go back," she said.

"Go back where, Miss Bibo?"

"To Germany, at least." She moved closer. Her round child eyes took him in with sudden trust. "But they think that's an insult."

Franz said nothing.

"With certain people charity is a hobby," she said.

"Yes," Franz said. He could see into Miss Bibo's room—a chipped iron bedstead, and on her wall a picture of Jesus pointing to His bleeding heart. A rag curtained her pantry, he saw, and the smell drifting from her room was Miss Bibo's smell of cooked cabbage and sweet perfume.

As he turned to go he heard Mozart's offertory, "Alma Dei

Creatoris." The music came from behind a dismal-looking door by the staircase. He stood transfixed. A boys' choir, supported by a small orchestra, sang the old Latin words he himself had sung as a boy in Prague, in the Monastery Church of Emaus. They sang very well, with a nice swing. In the gloomy hallway their voices sparkled, striking his senses like a chest of diamonds opened in the sun.

"That's Mr. Oliver," Miss Bibo said. "He owns this house. I wish he would play something else, for a change. Have you met Mr. Oliver?"

"No."

"He was looking for you. He wants someone who can read Czech."

The boy soloist held the line beautifully, carrying the melody, and the choir repeated it.

"You don't have to help Mr. Oliver, if you don't want to," Miss Bibo said.

"Don't you read Czech?" Franz asked.

"I am Hungarian," she said. "Besides, Mr. Oliver has very personal letters from Czechoslovakia, since the invasion. It is," she raised a dirty fingernail to her lips, "a matter of the heart."

Franz smiled and nodded. He could have meant yes or no.

On his way up he paused on the staircase as the choir and orchestra surged into the ravishing climax. *There sits the dear Mother of God the Creator, and the most merciful Mother of the guilty sinner. Mericiful One, make us, as we request, strong for the battle.* Then the music ended and silence flowed back through the house. Miss Bibo had closed her door, he saw, and Oliver's door, sunk in darkness, looked oddly askew and uninviting.

In his room, Franz sat down to the evening hours. When the lights came on in the street he closed his American History and sat by the window and looked into the street. A cold wind had blustered all day. The pavement was empty of pedestrians, the streetlamp shone feebly in the dusk, and squalls of fine snow flew over the parked cars.

His affair with Cynthia Garnet was over—if you could call it an affair. What had driven him away, Franz supposed, was his sense of her unhappiness, which made her face too long. Always looking dazed and sick as if she had just emerged from solitary confinement, she had spoken too superficially about the theater and dropped too many names to be more than a drifting hanger-on who had nothing better to do. He would have had the devil of a time extricating himself, if he'd made love to her.

He had kissed her twice, doubtfully, as if tasting sweets in a candy shop. Rejected, Cynthia Garnet had haunted his doorstep on East 110th, ambushed him in his office at Columbia, lain in wait for him in the lobby of International House. They had sat in the cafeteria, sipping coffee, lapsing into awkward silences, her long bony fingers pulling at a thread in her scarf. He could understand. She had offered herself, and he had not taken. "You're all talk, Franz," she had said, her mouth twisting unpleasantly. "I wonder if you know how really despicable you are."

In the end, Franz had gone to the housing office in the International House to look for another room. To get away from her. He had found nothing he could afford in Manhattan, but a landlord in Brooklyn was requesting a Czech tenant, and the rent was ridiculously low. So here he was, safe and sound with his stereo headphones and Mozart records. He did not need affairs. At thirty-five he needed a woman he could live with.

But Cynthia Garnet had persisted. Not knowing where he had moved, she addressed letters to him in care of Columbia's Department of Slavic Languages, where he taught two courses. He had picked up four of her letters with his check, and sorting them by dates discovered that she had written every day. "At least see me when I'm good," she said in her fourth letter, in which she enclosed a theater ticket—one ticket—and invited him to her performance. Leading lady or maid? he wondered. Off-Broadway, he noticed, studying the ticket, and debated whether to go or not.

Between then and yesterday he had received twenty-eight more letters from Cynthia Garnet. These, plus the first four, made thirty-two. He had counted them yesterday, sitting in his room on Myrtle Avenue, the stereo headphones clapped to his ears. Thirty-two letters.

If he'd come upon a packet of such letters from an unknown

woman to an unknown man, he would have thought them uninteresting. "If my love oppresses you, I don't want to be your love. I won't breathe a word of love. I am not asking you to love me. I know I have no claims, no rights to you."

What do you owe a woman for thirty-two letters? You owe her something, surely? He had snapped a rubber band around her letters, and, adjusting the headphones, reclined in the frayed armchair and closed his eyes, feeling happy. Mozart's *andante* was beginning.

Now, sitting in that same armchair, he watched the snow falling. Cynthia Garnet's performance was tomorrow. He would go to the theater, he decided, and tell her how good she had been, whether maid or leading lady.

A knock sounded on the door. Franz turned from the window and sat still.

The knock sounded again, timidly. Franz opened the door. The corridor was dark and his first view of Oliver was indistinct. What he saw was big and fat and stooped and shifting.

"The landlady—" said a soft voice, pitched high.

"Mr. Oliver? Come in, please."

The visitor advanced to the threshold and looked into the room. His face was round and flabby, forty-five years old perhaps, and his eyes were small and colorless and swerved slowly.

He said, as he looked about, "Can you read Czech and German?"

"Yes, of course."

"I'll pay you."

"Don't mention payment," Franz said. "Please come in."

"I have some letters in script, too," Oliver said. He came into the room then, a large clumsy body, and turned this way and that until Franz closed the door and showed him the old armchair.

Oliver sat down on the edge and put a manila envelope on his knees. "Here are the letters," he said. His fat hands crawled into the mass of papers and worried about in the deeps, and his thick lips worked along from above. "I am trying," Oliver said as he examined one letter after another, "to find something short to begin with. An example of each, maybe."

"You have many letters there."

"I have more downstairs," Oliver said. He smiled and his smile went deep into him and came back to his face. And his ears grew larger and he looked happy. He said, "These are just for the last six months."

"How is it you haven't had them translated before?"

"I would have come sooner," Oliver said. "But today was my dancing lesson." He counted on his fingers: "I study three courses at the Y.M.C.A. Monday, Film History, Tuesday, United Nations Relations, and Thursday, Dancing. Three courses."

"You keep yourself busy."

"Well, I just got back from Miami." Oliver smiled, but this time the smile played only with his mouth and the fat lips closed and rolled together complacently. "Here is a short letter," he said, holding up a page of rustling onionskin. "This one is from Hannelore. See if you can read it."

Franz took the page. A sharp, deeply blue ink had been used. It was a round exaggerated hand, starting evenly but at the end of each line crowding nervously.

Franz said, "Would you like me to read it word for word?"

"Just see if you can read it. Tell me what she says."

Oliver had fished out his whole treasure and was putting half of it back into the manila envelope.

Franz turned to the letter and read.

Hannelore said, Very honored Mr. Oliver, Your kind interest has overwhelmed me. I hasten to answer your questions. Number one, I have not received your promised parcel yet, but when I do I can assure you, dear Mr. Oliver, it will be a holiday for me. Number two, my favorite colors are red, blue, and yellow. I suppose black would be the most practical in our present circumstances, there being such a scarcity of clothing. But then black, since you ask to know my favorites, is not one of my favorite colors. Number three, my greatest need at the moment is a pair of shoes and a winter coat. The weather in the Erz Gebirge is something, I can assure you, and as we have scarcely enough fuel for cooking we are obliged to wrap ourselves in whatever comes to hand. A pair of shoes, then, and a coat would be like a miracle from heaven. Number four, my measurements are as follows: bust 99 cm, waist 74 cm, hips 108 cm. Number five, I enclose the photograph you requested. I do hope, dear Mr. Oliver, that I please you. And this brings me to your last question, number six. Yes, I do feel I could love you very much. I would make it my business to be the most devoted, efficient wife a man ever had. I feel much love for you already. I can see your generosity and kindness. If you can arrange for me to leave this country and come to America, you may be sure of receiving me as your most dutiful wife.

With much esteem, Hannelore.

Franz put down the letter.

Oliver said, "Now here is a letter from Magda, and this one is from Annie. I can't find Annie's first two letters. What did Hannelore say?"

Franz looked at Hannelore's letter. He heard Oliver wiggle himself into the comfort of the armchair. "She says," Franz said, "you have overwhelmed her with your kindness. She answers your questions. Her favorite colors are red, blue, and yellow . . . Would you like me to translate just as she has written?"

"Thank you, that's enough," Oliver said. He turned in the armchair and faced a bowl of apples on Franz's dresser. "I only want to know if we can continue with this."

Franz looked at him. He said, "Would you like an apple?"

"I like apples, but I don't eat them very often. They get stuck between my teeth." But he took an apple and sat back with a grunt. "Will you try Magda's letter next?"

Franz took the second letter from Oliver's hand. "Shall I read it out loud this time?"

"Yes, all right."

There were two sheets of dark-white notebook paper. Magda's hand was big and sloppy and presently jumped recklessly.

"She writes," Franz said, "Dear Oliver, I am so excited I cannot sit still, not for a moment! How could I dare hope that I would please you! I am now, you may well imagine, the happiest girl in all Prague! Perhaps I shall no longer have to watch the trains go without me?

Forgive me, but I feel I may speak freely, as you yourself suggest."
Here, Magda switched to the familiar *ti.* "You want a photo of me in
a bathing suit? Naughty boy! Believe me, nothing would please me
more. Unfortunately, I have no such picture at the moment. The
winter is harsh. But I shall make it my first duty in the spring to run
to the river and pose, my darling, just for you."

Oliver sat deep in the armchair. He nibbled the skin off the apple,
spat it into the ashtray, and, as Franz continued to read, explored
the soft fruit with his teeth.

"Are you really sending me parcels? Regularly? I kiss you for
them now, as if I had already received them. Will you be sure to include soap, chocolate and tobacco, and fats if possible. Yes, I can
dance—rather well, I am told! I measure 88, 66, 93." On the margin
Oliver had penciled the numbers 35, 26, 37. "My favorite colors are
yellow and white. As for clothes, I like them all! Bolts of cloth? Dear
God, I would faint, I swear it, if you sent me some silk! If you should
send me a nightgown for the summer I would like it in sheer white. If
you cannot find my exact size you may safely send whatever is avail-
able. My seamstress can do wonders! Will you write to me very soon,
dear Oliver? How I wish you were here! I would show you a thing or
two! Or three? I would like to say more but it is hard to write in this
cold room. With greetings and kisses and please write soon to your
adoring Magda."

Oliver took Magda's letter.

"They can't leave Czechoslovakia any more," Franz said.

"They can if you marry them," Oliver said. He stuffed Magda's
letter back into the manila envelope. "They become American
citizens. I'm not talking about Magda. A vulgar girl like that doesn't
deserve anything. I know her kind. She's older than she pretends to
be. And she'll take you for all you've got, and then some. But there
are good girls like Annie here. That's a different ball game."

"Don't you like American girls?"

Oliver bit into the apple and munched slowly. "Well," he said, "I
belonged to the Lonely Hearts Club for a while. That's in
Manhattan. But I want a foreign wife. I had a friend at International
House to help me, but he's gone now."

"He wrote to these girls for you?"

"No, he was already married. I get just as good results by myself. English is the international language over there."

Franz sat looking at him.

"See, you have to belong to this International Correspondence Club," Oliver explained. "White, black, yellow—anything you want. My club was the first to crack the Iron Curtain in Czechoslovakia." He pulled out a greasy wallet and showed Franz a membership card. It pictured hands clasped in friendship over the globe of the earth. The card was signed by a president and a vice-president, Los Angeles, California. "I'm a lifetime member," Oliver said, putting away his membership card. "That gives me first choice, like with Annie."

Oliver wanted to marry Annie and bring her over. If Annie did not want to stay married he would gladly divorce her and let her work around the house.

"You think that's immoral—to marry and divorce like that?" Oliver asked.

"No, no."

"I'd be marrying Annie to get her out of that country. She really deserves it."

"Is that Annie's letter?"

"What's wrong with that?" Oliver said defensively, as if Franz had disagreed. "Isn't it like Jesus healing the sick on the Sabbath? When all the hypocrites were saying how can you break the law of the Sabbath?" He had evidently thought long about Annie, and figured and planned. "I'd give Annie a hundred dollars plus room, same as Miss Bibo," Oliver said. "That's a lot of money to these people."

"Are you sure Annie would agree to it?"

"Oh, yes," Oliver said. "It's my hobby—helping people."

Franz crossed the room to the dresser and set the alarm clock for six-thirty. Noticing his stereo headphones, he stared at them for a moment.

"That way, Miss Bibo could go on Welfare and everybody will be happy," Oliver said. "That's all she's been talking about for ten years—going on Welfare."

Franz asked, standing by the dresser, "You brought Miss Bibo over? From Hungary?"

"Not like Annie. She thinks she fooled me. Say, listen, let me tell you something! Can I?"

"Sure."

"I may not be a genius, but I learned one thing in life. Patience. You understand?"

Franz nodded.

"That's all. Patience. I'd never lay a hand on Miss Bibo, no matter what she did to me. Words will never hurt me. I just want to see her face the day I bring Annie through that door."

"You wanted a wife—when you brought Miss Bibo over?"

"Not a wife. It was my moral obligation, that's all. You can't think right if you don't do right. Try and make *her* understand that!"

"How was it your moral obligation?"

"The Hungarian Revolt. You remember the Hungarian Revolt? If you wanted to save anybody you had to do it yourself."

He had gone too far, Franz realized. He did not want Oliver's confessions. No telling where they might lead. To change the subject, he said, "I heard you playing Mozart."

"Say! *You* like Mozart?" His voice took on a liquid softness, tenderness. "You think they beat those kids, maybe?"

"Beat them?"

"How do they get kids to sing like that? That's what I want to know."

Because, Oliver explained, that kind of music needs discipline, and children are naturally spastic. "That's a medically proven fact," he insisted, as Franz, in his growing wonder at the man, gave him a doubtful look. Oliver hastened to qualify: "I'm not saying those kids are *tortured*—though, who knows? Do *you* know all the secrets of the Catholic Church?"

"I'm sure I don't," Franz said.

"Priests do, and they're leaving the Church in droves—twenty-two thousand last year. They get drunk, wearing those black skirts. They can't marry, and yet they've got the world's largest library of dirty books in the Vatican."

The Church seemed clapped together in Oliver's brain from tabloid headlines and sectarian pamphlets.

And what about the catacombs *under* the Vatican? Oliver went on, warming to the subject, his breathing a touch labored. They used to castrate boys to make them sing like girls, didn't they? "Historical fact." Suppose, now, the cardinal brings his problem to the pope: "We've got this song by Mozart, Holy Father, but our little boys must be disciplined to do it right. We can't castrate them in our day and age. The law would get us on that one." Wouldn't the pope suggest some old-fashioned discipline? Set an example for parents. Kids are smoking pot and breaking windows, and burning the flag, and showing all manner of disrespect. There are ways and ways to terrify children. A cardinal who collects fine china, say, and knows more about precious stones than a Dutch jeweler, would appreciate a child's helplessness as a subject for artistic contemplation. Song can be tortured from a child's throat, pure and melodious, as art is tortured from the artist. Makes one giddy to hear such angels.

"I'm not saying that's how they do it," Oliver concluded. "I'm saying they must be doing *something* right . . . Can you read Annie? She's a doll! I would really marry her."

After a moment's hesitation, Franz took the letter and sat down. It was a lovely little hand, he saw, like a row of flowers.

"Honorable Mr. Oliver," Franz read abruptly. "You ask to know my favorite colors, my measurements, who this Mr. Kral is, whether or not I love you, and the affidavit. It is a sensitive position, dear Mr. Oliver, that gives truth the sound of ingratitude. If it will seem to you that in encouraging this correspondence I have put you in a false position, I beg you most earnestly to forgive me, I did not mean to deceive. It may be, when we exchanged our first letters, that I lost myself to a romantic mood. But now your gifts and kind requests have stirred in me a whirl of contrary feelings and memories.

"You desire me to sign an affidavit of your support, so that you can arrange my passage to the United States. What will you say to my answer but what is commonly said, that any girl in her right senses would be mad to refuse such an offer. Certainly I would like to see America. I would like, if that were possible, to come for a visit, so that we might get acquainted and perhaps become good friends; and if love beckoned, I should follow. You say you have been deceived once before—"

Franz stopped reading.

"They send you photographs of themselves when they were eighteen," Oliver said. "It's an old trick."

"You say you have been deceived once before," Franz read. "I am sorry, and the more reason for me not to sign your affidavit or promise to become your wife. Dear, dear Mr. Oliver, have you forgotten that I am a cripple? While my legs are paralyzed my arms have rather too much life in them! You can imagine how comical a figure I would cut in your house. Nor do I have a family to speak for me. My mother closed her eyes last year, and my father died the death of a hero on the field of honor, in the Great War. I am alone, you see, and but for Mr. Kral I would have fallen too."

"Do you believe that about Mr. Kral?" Oliver put in.

Franz opened his mouth, as if he needed air. He crossed over to the window and pulled down the shade. "What about Mr. Kral?"

"Keep reading," Oliver said. "She's going to talk about him now."

Franz went back to his chair, and continued:

"Mr. Kral is sixty-seven years old, a master carpenter. Like me, he has lost everything. He makes beautiful chairs and tables, and bookshelves and birdhouses, and he carves pictures of fields and rivers and pictures of hunters coming out of the woods. Mr. Kral made for me a little oak box with a hinged cover and a real silver padlock with a tiny key, and it really works, locks and unlocks, and although I keep nothing in it I treasure this box above all my possessions. Nowadays there is not much demand for Mr. Kral's lovely birdhouses.

"I cannot believe, dear Mr. Oliver, that my dimensions will interest you.

"Will you forgive me if I mention, if export to your country becomes permissible, and if you have friends who love birds and wish to house them, they will be able to send for the most beautiful nests in the world to Mr. Kral, who will dispatch them immediately at a very reasonable price.

"Your grateful friend, Annie."

Franz stared at the letter.

"I can't seem to find Annie's first two letters," Oliver said.

"Maybe some other time," Franz said.

When Oliver had packed away his letters, he rose to his feet with the manila envelope under his arm, and produced his wallet and opened it. "How much will that be?"

"No, please. Nothing."

Oliver pulled out a dollar, not all the way out. "You sure? Next time I'll bring you something. Maybe a bottle of wine?"

Franz opened the door for him. Oliver peered out and stepped back into the room. "Will that be all right?" he said. "A bottle of wine?"

"No, really—"

"I just don't understand why Annie had to lie about her arms."

"Arms?"

"Well," Oliver said, his effeminate voice feebly indignant, "it isn't likely, is it, that her legs should be paralyzed and not her arms?"

"Maybe it is so."

"Certainly not. Her legs are paralyzed, that's true, but so are her arms. Both her legs and arms are dead. She's completely helpless."

Franz held the door.

"Sure," Oliver began to smile. "It's a scientifically proven fact. Spine injuries, for example."

"Why do you think so, Mr. Oliver?"

"Could she write like that if she never went to school?"

"Did she say she never went to school?"

"How could she, if she is paralyzed? I bet she can't even spell."

Franz too began to smile. "How did she write the letter, then?"

"She didn't," Oliver said. "Mr. Kral would have to write it, wouldn't he, if her arms are dead? I'm not saying Annie didn't give him the general idea, maybe, but did you notice how he sneaked in his commercial?"

"I hadn't thought of that," Franz said.

Oliver acknowledged the compliment with his special smile. He smiled as he had smiled the first time, the smile that went deep into him and came back to his face, and again his ears grew larger and he looked happy.

Next day, in the evening, Franz went to the theater in the Village and found the house packed. And when the lights dimmed and the curtain rose, he understood the import of Cynthia Garnet's invitation. He sat far back, row K center, and watched her performance with astonishment. On stage, she was beautiful.

She was, after all, an actress. Gone was her emaciated look, her hollow cheeks, her sick pallor, and the tortured expression that made you think she staggered through life under impossible burdens. Not haggard now, but young for a woman of thirty, without a trace of bitterness or reluctance to live. She played her part with fine humor and an edge of elegant condescension. Even her dark soulful pleading eyes, which in her apartment had mildly irritated him, flashed mocking glances, intelligent and amused. Her walk was sprightly, her gestures were decisive, and her laughter sounded free and natural instead of strained and uncertain.

She offered love? Watching her, he drew a deep breath and crooked his index finger over his lips, and swore to himself that he could love the girl. Who could not love an illusion? She wore no makeup, if he could trust his eyes from row K. Under the stage lights her skeletal features composed an adorable face with a few strong lines, and she flounced about in her costume—a Cossack's cap and cape trimmed with fur—with the pretty delight of a child and a child's cruelty, with an air of indifference to whatever was dreary and dull and unoriginal, as befitted one so gifted. Love or not, Franz felt a passion for her, no doubt about it. Cynthia conveyed the sort of self-sufficiency that breaks men's hearts. On stage, she was beyond his reach, untouchable.

But this creature was not the real Cynthia Garnet, of course. He could not think of a woman he had taken to bed whom he could not love from row K in this theater, nor one with whose morning bleariness and cracked lipstick he could live. Cynthia Garnet's performance was enchanting, but *she* was not enchanting. How could she be enchanting in this theater and not in her apartment? Theatrical tricks don't change a woman. Do you love a woman because she plays the piano or dances on a tightrope? Love her in the Village but not on West End Avenue?

She got four curtain calls. As he clapped his hands the old emptiness froze him again. He had to fight off an impulse to leave the theater without seeing her. Say what you will, he argued with himself, such a performance deserves congratulations. So when the aisle began to clear he made his way backstage. People crowded the doorway to her dressing room and he could see heads milling about inside, under a pall of tobacco smoke. Half an hour later, when the guests began to leave, she noticed him skulking in the doorway. She flew to him and wrapped her arms around his neck and kissed him with hysterical force. "Stay to the end! Please?"

He nodded, smiling as if in pain.

"What a funny face you have!" she laughed, pulling him into the room. "Did you get my letters?"

He tossed his hand in a gesture of helplessness.

"I didn't expect you to answer, silly," she said. "You won't run away, now?" She introduced him to her friends, and a bald-headed man with a silk scarf gave him a plastic cup of champagne.

He leaned against the wall beside the dressing mirror, watching her as she flitted among her friends. He ought to leave. That would teach her not to send him one ticket, instead of two, for her performances. But he kept his place by the wall, sipping the champagne, following her with mistrustful eyes. And when all the guests had departed and Cynthia Garnet had withdrawn to the bathroom, Franz sat alone on the couch. She turned on the shower, he could hear. What was she doing? Repairing her face? Changing into seductive lingerie? He should steal away now, he thought.

His overcoat was missing from the chair where he had dropped it. He found it in her closet; she had hung it on a hanger. He yanked it off and sat on the couch with the coat on his lap, waiting to say good-by.

When at last Cynthia emerged from the bathroom, not in silks and nylons but a sack of a bathrobe and a towel wrapped around her head, she apologized for keeping him so long. "I just couldn't stand my hair another minute!" she said, and took his hand. "Hi."

She could not have made an entrance with less regard for herself. An actress knows her face. With her hair bunched up under the towel, her face was left to fend for itself, unframed, unprotected. She looked hideous. Her smile shifted her jaw out of line, and one ear seemed lower than the other, attracting attention to its utility. Her face would have intrigued an engineer. The salience of her eyesockets, the cheekbones, the jaws protruding at the hinges beyond their natural limits, as if for double reinforcement, thereby deepening the hollows of her cheeks—all these physical exaggerations which on the stage had composed her enchanting sweetness, breathing a pleasing fiction, here presented not so much a face as a frightful structure of bones. The human skull. An expert was needed to pronounce her male or female. She tilted her head, fixing him with her living eye. He pulled away his hand and hugged his overcoat.

"You were magnificent," he said. "I saw only you on that stage. I meant to bring you flowers, in fact. Do you like roses?"

Something about his look, or his tone, or his whole attitude, caused her to put a hand over her mouth to suppress laughter.

"God, why do I love you!" she said, embracing him. "That's all I've been asking myself. Why do I love an idiot like you!"

He stared at her.

"Poor baby, how can you give me roses?" she said, kissing him. "You don't see me at all. You don't see anybody, monster!"

"Then why are you kissing me?" he said, leaning away.

"Because you are a monster. If you ever met yourself you'd run screaming! You are ignorant and conceited and sentimental, and lost and lonely. That's why I love you. I love you because you're an idiot. My love is the best thing that's ever happened to you, and you want to throw me away?"

"You may call me anything you like," he said. "But you can't call me sentimental."

"Is *that* what's bothering you!" she laughed. "But that's exactly what you are, darling—sentimental. Through and through!"

"How? Where?"

"In your stinking room, that's where. Is it in Brooklyn?"

He remained silent.

"It figures," she said. "All alone, you can be sentimental to your heart's content, you and your Mozart."

He gave her a thin smile. "You think Mozart is sentimental?"

"Mozart isn't sentimental. You are. Don't get upset, sweet. You know more about Mozart than I'll ever know, but you've got this thing about him. Like people with one thing in their heads, all they ever talk about. They run into this thing and that's when everything stops for them. They get caught, or something, and can't get free, and you meet them five years later and they're still at it, telling you all about it, like they haven't lived a day since you last saw them. I once knew a professor like that. He had a thing about D. H. Lawrence. You'd think the world started and stopped with D. H. Lawrence. I hated his guts."

That pushed him into a deeper silence.

"Come on!" she said cheerfully. "Let's get out of here! We need to talk, don't we? Let's go to Gino's and talk. All right, Franz?"

But he would not be held. He must go home to his room on Myrtle Avenue.

"You stupid stick-in-the-mud!" she said.

Riding the subway, he slumped in his seat. The hurtling coach raised a storm of noises, creaks and squeals and fetid wind.

Her letters stopped, at any rate, and when she had not written for a week he began to relax.

On Friday evening he heard Oliver playing his "Alma Dei Creatoris" for an hour, over and over, and on Saturday Oliver started his musical orgy after lunch and did not stop until supper, when he went out. Franz tried Anti-Noise Ear Stopples—"Shut Out Noise . . . And Sleep Soundly!"—but the music pounded inside his head and plagued him in the street and the subway, and he would even catch himself humming the accursed tune. He had hours of respite, peace and quiet in his head, when he managed to forget Oliver, but coming and going the sight of Oliver's door by the staircase, when no sound came from within, sufficed to trigger his mental choir and orchestra into a fresh outburst.

At the age of thirty-five, in short, Franz became a puzzle to himself. He understood nothing any more. It was as if he had lived his life with a stranger and only now awakened to that fact. A stranger to himself, his hand shook in the restaurant as he brought the coffee cup to his lips, and in the drugstore he hesitated endlessly over trifuling choices.

Strangest of all, when he went to Columbia to pick up the week's junk mail and found a letter from Cynthia Garnet, the mere sight of Cynthia's letter started that damnable music in his head. "Alma Dei Creatoris" burst forth in its full Oliverian glory, and he felt congealing on his face, as he shoved Cynthia's letter into his pocket, Oliver's peculiar smile.

Letter number thirty-three. He did not read it then and there, nor on the subway, but waited until he had tiptoed past Oliver's door—a light showed in the crack—and gained the privacy of his room on Myrtle Avenue. The music in his head had stopped.

He listened. Below, Oliver was silent too.

Yet even then Franz could not open Cynthia's letter, but squirmed inwardly with the crawling sensation that Oliver had followed him into the room and now stood behind the armchair, peering over his shoulder. Irrationally, Franz turned to look. Nothing—except his stereo headphones on the dresser.

In this particular he understood himself well enough. What he could not endure was the indignity of reading Cynthia's letter through Oliver's eyes. He reviewed the obvious differences between Oliver and himself, and made a reasoned effort to detach himself from Oliver. But no matter how he twisted and shrugged and glared at the door, Oliver's spirit would not leave the room.

Slowly, he tore open the envelope. It was only a short note, but when he had read it he felt exhausted.

"Darling, I thought I would let you rest a while, to lick your wounds and recover your dear nerves. But now it is time to get back to work. You must know, I have no intention of failing you. One thing is clear to me. I will not let thee go, except thou bless me. Shall we begin? Please call me."

Eyes closed, he reclined in the armchair, his body inert, at rest. Nothing troubled him, nothing agitated. He had the pleasant sensation of drifting in a pacific dream, upon a tide bearing him softly out to sea. On the threshold of slumber, he heard a footstep by his door.

His eyes clicked open. He knew, as if he could see through the door, that Oliver was standing there, hesitating. Franz lay in the armchair, watching the door. After a long silence came the knock, timidly.

Franz opened the door.

"Are you busy?" Oliver said, standing sideways.

He shuffled into the room and settled himself in the armchair.

"I keep meaning to bring you a bottle of wine," he said, "but I don't know what you want. Is there any special wine you like?"

"That's all right. Please don't trouble."

"I want to ask you something," Oliver said.

Franz waited.

Oliver said, "Can you read *between* Annie's lines?"

"How do you mean?"

"Deductive logic." Oliver hunched forward. "Look here. We know Annie is paralyzed, right? She's as helpless as one of my Vienna Choir Boys. Secondly, she says she doesn't want to leave Czechoslovakia. Isn't that interesting? Because there's Russians all around her, right? I wouldn't be surprised if a Communist is sitting in her room right now, drinking tea. Say he takes off her shoes and plays with them. What could she do?"

Franz pulled up a chair and, for the first time, watched Oliver without aversion, with clinical interest.

"I mean," said Oliver, "how do you see Annie?"

"I don't know—beautiful, I think."

"Wouldn't you call her a masochist? If she doesn't want to be saved, doesn't it mean she wants to be helpless? At the mercy of anybody walking into her bedroom? They can do anything they like to her. That's what she wants!"

"All right. Suppose it is so."

Oliver looked about for the bowl of apples. It was gone. "I've been thinking," he said. "She could get the best psychiatric treatment right here in New York. If she'd only let me bring her over."

"How can you save her if she doesn't want to be saved?"

"She might if you wrote to her, in your own language. She'd answer you. I'll give you ten dollars."

"Mr. Oliver—"

"It's worth it to me. I'll give you the general idea. You just put it in your own language, with your politeness. She'll listen to that."

Fat and shabbily dressed, Oliver sat waiting for Franz's answer with a begging look.

"I can't help you, Mr. Oliver."

"Don't you believe Annie needs help?"

"I'm sorry. I can't do this."

"Don't you want to help Annie?"

"I'm really too busy."

"Oh, boy," he said, smiling at Franz. "You want more money? Is that it?"

"No." Franz stood up, to show that the interview was over.

"I think ten dollars is fair. But I'll make it fifteen, if you insist. You know how I feel about Annie."

"I know."

Oliver picked himself up and lumbered to the door. "I wouldn't have come if you hadn't invited me. Just remember that."

"Of course. I'm sorry."

Oliver backed away in the dark corridor, his hulk sharply outlined against the light from the stairwell. When he had reached the staircase he stood breathing for a moment. They looked at each other and spoke quietly over the distance between them.

"Can I ask you one question?" Oliver said.

"Sure."

"Did somebody help *you* out of Czechoslovakia?"

"Yes, as a matter of fact."

Franz could not see the expression on Oliver's face. It was hidden in shadows. Oliver's whole body was a mass of breathing darkness. "That's all I want to know," he said, and vanished down the stairwell.

For a long time Franz sat in his room, his hand pressed to his mouth. Then he pulled on his winter coat and went downstairs, and when he saw Oliver's door the sacred music started in his head, as vividly as if he could hear it with his ears. The melody from which all waste, all vanity, all pretensions had been burned away by the master's art, could bear no further refinement. Pure and flawless, it flowed from the throat of a tortured child begging forgiveness with exquisite tears.

Miss Bibo's door stood closed, he saw, and her threshold showed no light. In the dark vestibule his face was struck by the street air, cold enough to ventilate a tomb, and as the door creaked shut behind him the whole choir in his head burst out in horror, wonder, and adoration, *"Mater, mater clementissima!"* With a shiver, he turned up his collar and pushed out into the night, to the drugstore to call Cynthia Garnet, and walked in the winter slush feeling heavy-laden, a man in the middle of his journey.

Demons

Sasha Kuznetsov, thirty, with overgrown curly hair and large dark eyes, who after the war had been transported from a German DP camp to Chicago by a charitable Christian association, rose at noon without waking the girl he had slept with, yawned, hitched up his long white cotton nightshirt, and climbed on the table under the basement window to unfasten the window guard, as he called it. He himself had made the window guard of plywood, acoustical tile, and cotton, all wrapped in green plastic, and lashed it to the barred window with ropes and hooks to muffle the noises of the street.

Lowering the contraption to the floor, he looked out over the sunlit, trashy pavement. *Scheise!* A parking ticket fluttered on the windshield of Jill's blue convertible. The billboard across the street, loyal to Schlitz for two months, had sold out in the night to Winston filter cigarettes. The Blue Tap on the corner had opened its door to the dust and car fumes drifting in the sunlight, and the tavern's fat, unshaven proprietor, in undershirt and suspenders, sat on his chair by the door, enjoying the spring.

The girl awoke. "Sasha?"

"The street is full of devils this morning," he said. He climbed down from the table, which was piled with books and periodicals. In the shaft of sunlight, his naked legs showed dark and hairy under his white nightshirt. "Jilly, your car has got a ticket," he said, sitting down beside her and falling to a brooding study of her face.

"I'll give it to Daddy."

Wearing a pink nightgown with white lace at the neck and sleeves, she sat up in the bed under Sasha's crucifix, kissed him, and lit a cigarette. Jill Smith-Lockwood had a delicate face and long yellow hair. She had driven her blue convertible from her home in Lake Forest to spend a creative weekend with Sasha, for she was a student at the Art Institute. There was her portfolio of drawings, on the upright piano, and her wooden box of charcoals, pencils, and bamboo sticks. Her near North Side friend, Genoveffa Sweeny, who called herself a professional model, covered up for her with her parents.

"I never get tired of you," Sasha said, fetching a sigh. "You are so beautiful!"

"Monkey! I want to run all the way to the lake! All right, Sasha?"

They would buy smoked chubs, wrapped in newspaper, in a fisherman's hut on the lake and eat them on the pier, watching the sun glinting off the scum on the water.

"We'll go," he said. "Tell me, when did you fall in love with me?"

"The moment I saw you."

"Because I am poor and humble?"

"You are neither poor nor humble. Come on, Sasha! It's past noon!"

When she was dressed in a yellow summer dress, she looked sixteen. Sasha, in sandals, pants, and shirt, sat at the table, reading his Bible. She kissed his neck, and said, "I loved you when you got lost in the gallery. I thought you were lying. You weren't . . . were you?"

Some months before, Genoveffa Sweeny had brought them together at the Lautrec show—"Don't either of you talk to me until you've slept together"—and they had wandered away from the show, talking, through corridors and rooms hung with paintings, and fallen to kissing on the leather couch under Seurat's "Jatte."

"I never lie to you, Jilly. It's my memory. Do you know this about the seven terrible spirits?"

"Please leave that black book. I'm starved."

"What does this mean? 'He drives out his bad spirit, and the spirit comes back with seven other spirits worse than himself.' "

Jill untied her portfolio and spread her drawings on the bed. When Sasha got an idea, he had to talk. He had another interesting peculiarity: when he told the truth about himself, he sounded like a liar. He had confessed, for example, that he gave up a salary of $20,000 at Stokely, Wimsatt & Pulsifer, an import-export firm, for a life of voluntary poverty. Besides the improbability of such renunciation, his manner of talking about it, the confused, tortured expression on his face as he tapped his forehead to coax his memory, his sudden smile as he remembered the names of his former employers, and dramatic gestures, told her that he was lying, when in fact he was telling the truth. Nor had he been fired: after six years with Stokely, Wimsatt & Pulsifer, he got an idea and quit. He had tasted success and spat it out of his mouth. "How much land does a man need?" Now, as night cashier in a Rush Street restaurant from midnight to 4:00, he had time to take in art shows and concerts, read his books, and wander from one to another of Chicago's colleges, studying whatever took his fancy—at the moment, dogmatic theology under Father Ignatius, who showed slides of the Shroud of Turin.

"Where have I read it?" Sasha said, rummaging through his books. He had forgotten Jill, who sat on his bed amid her drawings, watching him. "Father Ignatius says religion is good for all people. What do you think, Jilly?"

He might have gone on had not his landlady above, Mrs. Selig, struck the floor three times with the handle of her broom, to summon him to the phone. Grabbing his own broom, Sasha returned the signal, striking his ceiling three times, yelled, "I am coming, Mrs. Selig!" and ran out.

When he returned ten minutes later, Jill was gone. He found her on the street, sitting in her blue convertible. The sun was bright and hot.

"Jilly! What is the matter?"

"You seem to be very busy this weekend."

"Jilly!"

"I don't know about you, Sasha, but I am going to Stouffer's for breakfast. Right now!"

"I have a catastrophe. Please, come in at once. I must know what to do."

"You always have catastrophes. What's her name?"

"Oh, Jilly, no! Please, how can you think?" He looked up and down the street of shabby taverns and lurching noon drunks, and clutched his head. "This is terrible! Our weekend is shattered!"

"Oh?"

Her curiosity got the best of her, and she followed him back into his basement room. He shut the door, peered out the window, and turned to her with a wild look.

"All right, Sasha, who was it?"

"My brother."

He had never mentioned a brother. "*You* have a *brother?*"

"Nikolai. He called from the airport. He will be here in an hour."

Was he lying? "You never told me you had a brother."

"What shall I tell? For eight years, he writes at Christmas. Now he comes for one day to tell me about his success. I will be upset for a month."

"Is he younger than you?"

"No, no, I am the kid brother. He went to study, and now he is a great man. He will tell you." Sasha flung himself down beside Jill and took her hands. "Jilly, what do I want? A peaceful, quiet, humble existence. No more! The self must be uprooted!" He tapped his chest with his finger, to indicate what he was. "Neutrality!" he cried. "But he is all ego. Not aware of anybody, only himself. It is impossible to converse with him! You sit and listen, and he talks your head off for *hours!* Imagine, he thinks he is spiritual! A God-seeker!"

Sasha could not be inventing all this. "What does he do?" Jill asked.

"The crucifix!" Sasha cried. "If he thinks I'm a Catholic, he will preach all night!" He yanked the crucifix off the wall and shoved it into the oven. Next went the Bible from the table. Then he looked round to see what else to hide, and saw that the crucifix had left its mark on the whitewashed wall. He hung over it one of Jill's drawings—a nude—and stepped back.

"A work of art, after all. He cannot call it salacious. And what if he does? So much the better! Let him think I am lost in the gutters of Chicago, sunk in degradation and despair."

He brought a hand to his throat and stood frozen, suddenly, in stunned silence. "My God!" he breathed. "Nikolai must be nearly forty. Can you imagine? Wait, I am thirty, so he must be thirty-eight. Thirty-eight! Twelve more years, he will be fifty. Ten more, sixty, one foot in the grave!"

"Will you please calm down. I should think you would be happy to see your brother, after all these years."

"I *am* happy! If only he did not talk about religion! Then he becomes a madman. Oh, Jilly, Jilly, he will turn my peaceful, neutral room into a *church!* I feel I must take a bath afterward."

"Maybe he's changed. After all, you haven't seen him for eight years."

"Don't worry, he was like that ten years ago. Fifteen! He is crazy —I say it clinically. He has a Ph.D., he has money, he has everything."

She said, "Let's at least have some coffee. Then we can take your brother to Stouffer's for brunch."

"No!" he cried, horrified. "No, no, Jilly! I must not give him occasion. He will guess at once we are lovers, out of matrimony. Then he will never stop preaching."

"Is he all that religious?"

"A minister! He is not Nikolai Kuznetsov any more. Now he is Nicholas Cousin. Reverend Nicholas Cousin."

"What church does he belong to?"

"Not really a minister. He works for many churches on the East Coast. Wait, I am trying to think." Sasha put his hands over his eyes.

"But you just said he is a reverend," Jill said.

"A minister of education. He is an organizer. You know, young people? That's what he does—conventions, summer camps, tours. He travels all the time. By jet."

"How long is he staying?"

"Only till midnight, thank God. Can you give me $2.25?"

"What for?"

"Haircut. He will think I am a Beatle, when I am only poor. Then there will be more preaching."

After a moment's hesitation, Jill opened her purse and gave him the money. "What else?"

"Twenty-five cents more for tip."

She gave him another quarter. "Anything else?"

"Nothing else, my darling. Thank you! I shall give it back to you next Friday. Now you must go, quickly. Go to Gena, tell her about my brother. She will understand."

"I'll do that."

"You are my angel! I shall call you at midnight, as soon as he is gone. All right, Jilly?"

"What if he decides to stay overnight?"

"Impossible! He must be in New York in the morning."

Sasha saw her out to her blue convertible, gave her the parking ticket from the windshield, and stood on the pavement looking distracted as she started the engine.

"Jilly, Jilly, you are angry. Forgive me, he only comes once every eight years. Tomorrow, I promise, we go to the pier all day. Smoked chubs, and you can draw the Prudential. I will sing to you with my mandolin!"

"Sure."

"Now go, quickly! I shall call you at Gena's."

"Sasha."

"Yes, my heart?"

"I'll be back after midnight." And she drove off.

The street was dusty, hot, and glaring, hurting his eyes. The proprietor of The Blue Tap had left his chair by the door, and from within the dark tavern came the rhythmic thumping of the jukebox. Sasha hurried past the pawnshop to the barber.

Nikolai Ivanovich Kuznetsov, alias Nicholas Cousin, a well-fed, rosy-cheeked man of thirty-eight with a face Americans call good-looking, having a small straight nose and a thin hard mouth, kept the taxi driver waiting as he embraced his younger brother, who had come running from the house to greet him. Both broke into tears. Weeping, they held each other at arm's length, kissed again, and shouted each other's names.

"Let me pay your man!" Sasha cried in Russian, fishing about in

his pockets for money he did not have. "I insist! You are my guest!"
The barber had cut his hair short, lowering his ears and giving him a
goofy look as he grinned up at his brother.

"Nonsense," said Nikolai. He peeled off some notes from a roll of
money and paid the driver.

"I won't have you spending money while you are my guest!" Sasha
said. Arm in arm, they went into the house. Sasha took him in by the
front door, rather than by the back past the garbage cans. "A guest
is a guest!"

"I am on an expense account," Nikolai said in English.

As they passed the hallway mirror, each caught the other giving
himself a look. They went down a narrow, creaking staircase to the
basement and into Sasha's room.

"But this is charming!" Nikolai exclaimed. He looked round at
the bed, Jill's drawing of the nude above it, the books on the table,
the piano. "So this is how you live." He crossed to the window,
touched the books. "No, it's ideal! Ideal!" He struck a key on the piano, and thundered out the opening chords of the *Pathétique*. "My
God, I never imagined! You have everything one needs."

"Tea or coffee?"

"No, no, we'll go out. Have you eaten today?"

"I just got up, actually. I work in a restaurant from midnight to
4:00."

"He works in a restaurant and lives like a king! I've often thought
of doing the same, or even entering a monastery. A quiet, contem-
plative life. Is that your drawing?"

"No . . . a friend."

"Girl friend?"

"Yes, as a matter of fact. A student at the Art Institute."

"I'd give up everything!" Nikolai said, with sudden passion. He
moved close to have a better look at the nude. "She gave you this picture?"

"One of her better studies. She wanted me to have it."

"If I weren't so tied up with the churches . . . What is money? It's
filth!"

"How can you say that?" Sasha cried. "If I had your brains and education, do you think I would be living in this hole? I simply haven't the strength. You can't imagine how much I admire you, Kolya!"

"It's all vanity. But why are we standing here? Is there a good restaurant nearby?"

"We'd have to go to Michigan Avenue. But I don't want you to spend money."

"Filth and nonsense! You'll see how I can spend. Come along!"

By the time they had lunched at the Allerton, walked along the lake, and moved on to the Boul-Mich for vodka, they had lapsed into Russian. They sat in a dark corner of the bar, at a small round table, talking and waving their arms. Not a smoker himself, Nikolai tried one of Sasha's cigarettes, got drunk on that alone, and pulled from his jacket a news clipping: "*Cousin to Head Inter-Faith Youth in Adirondacks.*" He had become so well known in church circles in New York that an Eastern conference had approached him about organizing an evangelical tour of Soviet Russia, something on the order of a Billy Graham crusade.

"As if Russia needs them," Nikolai said, and burped. "You can see the irony. In Russia, the Fundamentalists are the most liberal group; here, they are the most reactionary."

"You did not tell them that?"

"Black on white. They can be squeezed like putty."

His head swimming, Sasha smiled at his brother through the tobacco fumes. "Do you know what I did when you called me from the airport?" He told him how he had removed his crucifix from the wall, and the Bible from the table.

"Go and look!"

"You haven't become a Catholic?"

"No, no. I read the Bible; it interests me. The crucifix is simply for mood."

"What mood?"

"A serene atmosphere. You know? I want a different tone from the street, that's all. I'll show you when we come back. My girl friend wanted to meet you."

"She was with you?"

"She comes on weekends. I chased her away."

"But why, you idiot? You have a mistress, then?"

"You could call her that, I suppose."

"Do you actually sleep with this girl?"

"Sleep, talk, go swimming—we are friends."

"That's wonderful! Tell me, is it hard to have women around here?"

"One meets them."

"How? On the street?"

They were still talking about women when they came out into the avenue, now crossed with long shadows. Sasha, a hand on his brother's neck, offered to call Jill, to ask if she and her friend, Genoveffa Sweeny, would meet them for a drink, and perhaps dinner afterward. The evening was warm, with a smell of the lake in the air, and the neons atop the skyscrapers blinked feebly in the setting sun.

"It's not the women," Nikolai said, as they walked unsteadily, side by side, into the revolving door of a drugstore, and somehow staggered through. They had wandered into a hotel drugstore with indirect lighting, soft music, and a short-order cook at the grill dressed in a white jacket with brass buttons. One of those odd women of fifty or sixty, excessively powdered and rouged, who come down from their rooms upstairs for a cup of coffee dressed in very tight black pants, sat at the counter, showing the length of her legs, a cigarette between her fingers and a poodle at her feet. The brothers stared at her face, which seemed made of fine old rubber, and turned to the phone booths.

"Wait," said Nikolai, stopping by a display of chocolate boxes. "This Genoveffa—I have no intention, you understand?"

"But why think about it? Such things happen or they don't, quite naturally."

"Is she . . . the sort?"

"If you hit it off, why not?"

"Women have never liked me," Nikolai said. "With you it's different. I can see that. You don't care what you do in life, you want to amuse yourself. That's what appeals to them." He gave a short, choppy laugh that sounded like a bark. "Am I right?"

"I suppose," Sasha said.

"You suppose. And yet it doesn't matter to you? If you sat on a dung heap instead of in a crystal palace, do you suppose you would know the difference? But that is just what appeals to women. They have a sixth sense; they know whom they can trust. Someone, you see, who does not know the difference. A man without inner struggles. With such a man they can be comfortable. Of course! They risk nothing!" He laughed again.

"Hm," said Sasha.

"You have someone like Goethe, someone like Pushkin, men with titanic struggles in their souls, they will be at once suspected by women. They all had unhappy love affairs. Tragedies!"

"Hm."

"If you can be comfortable in the mire with a woman, well and good. They, too, are comfortable then, and smother you. But if you can't, Sasha, if you can't!"

"Then you can't," Sasha said, venturing a smile.

"Then you can't. Then you must will only one thing—not to be a pig. When you've had God, you can never do without Him again. Here," Nikolai said, pressing his stomach with both hands, "and here," his chest. "Through every vein!" He raised his fist, and Sasha flinched. "As though the whole body were flooded with light! But when you've had a woman, you want to get rid of her. You don't want to see her any more."

The best thing you can do with a brother like that is to agree. That's not hard. Being younger, you owe him a certain deference; that is only natural. Besides, he'll grab you by the throat if you disagree, and strangle you for your own good. People who have found the Truth are dangerous. What is harder is to think of what to do with your brother until his plane leaves at midnight.

"Well," said Sasha, looking around the drugstore. The slender old woman with the rubber face had left. From behind his glass counter, the cashier, an old man with a crew cut, sat watching them. "Look, Kolya, we wouldn't have time for the girls, anyway. You must catch your plane at midnight."

"No, why? Call them, call them! We'll go anywhere you like, the best dinner. I can easily postpone my flight till tomorrow, even day after tomorrow.''

"But you have to be in New York tomorrow.''

"I'm not scheduled to speak. I'm a brilliant speaker, by the way. Can't you come and hear me sometime? You'll see.''

"I should like to.''

"No,'' said Nikolai, pulling him to the phone booths, "as long as I am here I want to see something of your life. To tell you the truth, I want to wallow in the mire myself, just to get it out of my system.''

"I'm not sure I can promise you a real mire,'' Sasha said timidly, hanging back.

"A little puddle will do.'' He pressed a dime into Sasha's hand for the toll call. "Call them! I'm not a mystic yet, heh-heh! Yet, do you know,'' he leaned close, "there are mystics in India who keep women in their monasteries, simply to rid themselves of the desire?''

"They sleep with them?''

"Whenever they like, and they never think or talk about sex. Why should they? Imagine, the government wants to suppress them for licentiousness, when in fact these monks fornicate with the purest of hearts.''

Where does he pick up such information? Sasha wondered, and did not know what to do with him.

What excited Nikolai's fancies was that Genoveffa Sweeny did not answer her phone. What could she be doing? Was she really as pretty as Sasha made her out to be? Did she actually take sex as lightly as a handshake? Did such girls exist in this wonderful city? Saturday night's festivities had begun. Music and laughter sounded from doorways, men and women drove by in taxis, and the air was charged with electricity. Anyone in Nikolai's condition could feel it. Then the brothers turned into Rush Street and, at sight of the discotheques and cabarets and key clubs coming alive with lights and a flurry of pretty faces, Nikolai declared that he wanted to taste the very dregs of Chicago's night life. A man ought to taste everything. He ought to know the depths of his own most degrading possibilities. Dante's journey to heaven led through hell. And, wherever the brothers paused for vodka, they saw beautiful women in life's most enchanting hour, in the first flush of the night's excitement—women in tights and tight dresses, with mysterious smiles and bewitching eyes. Arriving at a dark, expensive night club where a party was already in full swing, Nikolai would go no farther, like Balaam's ass. Here he would stay, in a crowd of beautiful sinners, and order dinner.

They had stumbled into a fascinating pit. The music was loud and mad. The musicians, slapping and blowing their instruments, writhed on their chairs like trained reptiles, the singer staggered about the microphone in an apoplectic fit, and the piano player seemed to be gnawing at the keyboard of the shuddering piano. On the dance floor, bodies jerked, legs flashed, bellies jiggled, backsides wiggled. It was enough to make one faint with delight.

"Freedom!" Nikolai said, his eyes glittering as he watched the dancers. "What do we know of freedom?"

He held his vodka very well; he did not slaver; but he was eager to strike up a conversation with a woman. However, when the waitress took their orders for steak and he saw that she wore nothing, evidently, but a bikini made of fish-netting, he addressed her with cold formality. "Medium rare, please."

"No, seriously," he said to Sasha, and scratched his neck furiously and tossed his head from side to side, as if in torment, before taking up his glass suddenly. *"Na z'darovye!"*

Sasha was half dead with vodka and could scarcely keep his eyes open. *"Z'darovye,"* he mumbled.

"It's a good fight! I can feel it! Look, there's another!" Nikolai turned to follow another waitress with his eyes, who also wore nothing but fish-netting and wove prettily among the tables, a tray on her naked shoulder. She disappeared behind a bamboo wall. "It's really a form of burlesque, isn't it?" he asked Sasha.

"I've never been here before."

"Strange, I don't feel in the least aroused. Do you?"

"No."

"I think it's because I look at them with a certain detachment," Nikolai said. "I look as an artist might—" He stopped in mid-sentence, his eyes wide. Their waitress was serving steak to the neighboring table, her back to the brothers. She spread her legs slightly to brace herself on her very high heels and bent low as she took the plates off her tray and set them carefully on the table.

"Oh, my God!" said Nikolai, when she had disappeared behind the bamboo wall.

Some complacent devil made Sasha say, "Genoveffa used to work in one of these clubs."

"Try them again, Sashinka. Here." Nikolai gave him a dollar. "Where is the phone? It's a pity to waste such a dinner without company. Go on, call them!"

"But she doesn't answer. They must have gone out."

"Try again! I will cancel my flight. I can fly tomorrow, next week—what do I care?"

Sasha stepped carefully among the tables, uttering apologies as he reached for the backs of chairs for support. In the phone booth, he fell promptly asleep. He awoke with a start, and dialed Genoveffa Sweeny's number. Again, there was no answer, and he made his way back to his brother. The floor show had come on. A young man in a dark suit sat on a high stool on the dance floor, a spotlight showing the powder on his face, and told jokes about the government. At their table, the steak had been served and Nikolai ate vigorously, slashing and chewing, ignoring the comedian.

"I tried them six times. I'm sorry," Sasha said. He felt refreshed and hungry after his nap in the phone booth, and fell to.

"Never mind, brother. I'm staying through tomorrow. We've had no time to organize. Tomorrow, we'll organize. She's sleeping with you tonight?"

"Well . . . I don't know."

When they left the club at midnight, too late to catch his plane, Nikolai walked moodily with his head thrust forward, looking for a stray woman on deserted Michigan Avenue. Sasha's horror at the money his brother had spent, his lie that he did not know Genoveffa Sweeny well enough to invite her into his basement, his truthful guess that she had already caught herself a lover for the weekend— nothing could dissuade Nikolai from the hunt. He had to have a woman before he left Chicago, where nobody knew him. A coarse young girl, for instance, who would kiss your foot for $10. Leaving the elegance of Rush Street, he made for the human scum on State Street, where anything might be possible.

There they gleamed and breathed, the shabby taverns that had the sour air of dark public latrines. The brothers had to step around drunks lying sprawled in dark doorways. They saw no women in these taverns, young or old. They saw only the bent backs and hairy arms of men, sitting stolidly at scratched counters under fly-catchers black with squirming flies. The Blue Tap, on Sasha's own corner, was the dirtiest of the lot. Here, the jukebox howled and a cripple in filthy pants shuffled before it, back and forth, a beer bottle in his hand, his face corrupting from some internal sickness.

Then Sasha saw, on the far side of the street, a light shining in his basement window, and Jill's convertible parked before his house. And in the next hour, as if by magic, the sexual adventure Nikolai had been seeking all day was offered him by Jill's friend, Genoveffa Sweeny, who had come to Sasha's room on a bet that his brother did not exist. She offered him the adventure easily, agreeably, and as naturally as one could wish. Did Nikolai intend putting up at the St. Claire? No need: Gena had a couch in her apartment, not five streets away. Besides, she did not dare go home at this time of night without escort.

In Sasha's room, Nikolai retreated behind polite manners, but Gena pursued him with hysterical laughter. She was a loud, uninhibited girl with a quick mind and such a direct style of attack that she embarrassed him. She flew at his shyness with sexy jokes, laughed loudly at his evasive answers, and affected a husky tone, setting her shoulders and breasts in voluptuous motion, her eyes fixed on his and her mouth twitching for her next laugh.

"Are you also a student at the Institute?" Nikolai asked her.

"They threw me out. I can't draw."

"Sure she can," Jill said. "She's just being modest."

"That's why I can't draw all those beautiful men. I'd much rather *be* drawn."

"Gena models for our life class," Jill explained.

"Really?" Nikolai said, clearing his throat.

"In the *nude!*" Gena said. Watching Nikolai's face, she laughed loud and long.

That broke Nikolai. And as he started to flirt openly, a change came over him. In Sasha's private world under the house, with two pretty girls sitting on the bed like apples in a bowl, joking about sex, Nikolai's sensuality seemed to awaken to its own sweet innocence as from a hideous dream. He looked happy for the first time that day. Gena may have been wild, but it was as though she were liberating Nikolai's desires.

Jill had brought beer and meant to serve it, but Sasha signaled to her with his mouth. She looked at him. *No? No!* he grimaced. He did not want to prolong the party. He was waiting for Nikolai to get some sense into his head and take the girl home, and call it a night. By the time he had pulled Jill away from her six-pack and seated her beside himself, he noticed that the tone in the room had subsided. Nikolai and Gena had stopped laughing and were talking earnestly, nose to nose.

"I think it's an adorable idea! All those beautiful young girls. May I come, too? If I promise not to be naughty?"

"You are joking."

"I swear it! I'll come to your church," she said, her lips gleaming like wet cherries, "if you come to mine."

"*Your* church?"

"My apartment, silly. You come to me, and I'll come to you. Ask Jill if I won't."

"Is she serious?" Nikolai asked Jill.

"Don't dare her," Jill said. "She just might."

"You know damn well I'm serious! I'll keep my part of the bargain, if he keeps his. What do you say, Nikolai? Do we kiss on it?" Their lips were close, almost touching.

"I'm an ordained minister," he said. "Do you understand what that means?"

"I want you more than ever. Sleep with me tonight, and I'll be your convert."

"Don't be crazy," Jill said. "She's teasing you. Stop it now, Gena!"

"He believes in God, doesn't he?" Gena said, without turning her eyes from him. "He actually and truly believes in God. Well, I believe in sex. Actually and truly. Is it a bargain, Nikolai?"

"Yes," he said, after a long pause. "But you must first become a Christian. Then we'll talk about sex."

"*Talk?* What kind of a deal is that?"

For some moments they sat there, face to face, holding hands, their knees pressing, like lovers.

"It's getting late," Sasha broke in. "What do you think, Kolya?"

"Past 2:00!" he said, glancing at his watch, and dropped Gena's hand. "I must be off. I hope I haven't kept you up too late."

If he found a taxi, he could make the 3:40 flight to New York, in good time for his conference in the morning.

I thought so! Gena's look said, as he pulled on his raincoat.

But, instead of leaving, Nikolai hesitated, struggled to master himself. Then he sat down.

"I want to do a service, before I leave," he said. "Before my journey." His tone showed that he was really begging her permission to render his service. He seemed to need Gena in his worship of God, as a moment before she had needed him in her worship of love. She sat stiffly on the bed. The color of laughter had drained from her face. "Will you bear with me?" he asked her.

"Go right ahead. Don't mind me."

"I want to sing a song and say a prayer. It won't take long."

Sasha sat tightly. Nikolai broke into his hymn without ado, his hands folded, his face turned to the window. "Now take my hand and lead me." There was something sad about the way he sang, in a sort of self-abasement compounded of shame and happiness. He sang without faltering, although he must have been painfully aware of Gena. But it was his turn, now, to reveal himself, to undress before her and show himself naked.

Sasha felt an inward hush as he listened to his brother. Praying the Our Father, Nikolai spoke the words without haste, at peace with himself, his head bent before Gena. Outside, from across the street, the jukebox thumped brutally in the night.

And when he had left the basement and was gone—well, they felt,

certainly he had done an odd thing. Nikolai's oddness lay heavy in
the room as the three sat there, trying to make up their minds about
him.

"He's grown worse," Sasha muttered, thinking about the unclean
spirit.

But to Gena his performance was a strange act of love. Strange,
but an act of love. In any case, as they were talking lightly again and
laughing, Gena burst into tears, quite unexpectedly, and would not
be calmed for a long time.

Longface

A car drove by in the rain and splashed his feet. He touched the wet cello case for the bow. It was there.

On the far side of the street another young man came out of a novelty shop, recognized Mark, and ran over. It was Bradley Walker, Mark saw with annoyance. Not since college, Bradley said, and four long years. They had not been close friends in college, but to Bradley Walker the passing of four years meant being in a far country, and he was hugging a fellow tourist.

Could they get out of the rain? Had Mark eaten? Bradley's car stood parked around the corner. What was he doing with a fiddle? Bradley himself had turned professional. Did he remember Bradley's column, "File 13," in *The Shaft?* Well, Bradley was writing copy for Sylvester Kellogg—Kellogg's Complete Creative Service. Kellogg knew technique when he saw it and paid very good money, by the way. Mark used to make witty jingles, Bradley remembered. Did he still make them?

"No."

Bradley laughed. "You haven't changed a bit. You're not playing in Orchestra Hall?"

"No."

Mark turned to see if the bus was coming. Rain. Bradley pulled at his arm. He did not have to go home yet, did he? A reunion, after all. After dinner at Le Bistro, Bradley would give him a ride home.

"You're not married?" Bradley asked.

Mark shook his head.

They turned the corner to Bradley's car, a new model that looked like a fish. Bradley flicked on the radio as they drove off. Pardon, but Mark did look run-down. Was he working or having a good time? Bradley was working and even thinking of getting married. Can't fool around all your life.

Mark enjoyed the car. He sat feeling the rain in his left shoe. His girl, Cathy, waited for him in his basement. She was cooking meat dumplings. There would also be cake and hot chocolate, she had promised, and green paper napkins to celebrate the start of a new life.

They drove to Le Bistro. As they went in, Bradley Walker clapped the doorman on the back. In the cloakroom he patted the cheek of a rouged woman who held her head like a camel. Under his coat Bradley wore the adman's uniform for that season, beige trousers and jacket buttoned very high. Could Mark eat a steak? A drink first? He led him to the bar.

"Can't they serve at a table?" Mark asked.

"Sure." But Bradley, touching his tie, saw a face at the bar and excused himself for a moment.

A hidden mechanical system in the dining room cooled in the cold autumn, and another system hummed music for everybody's dining pleasure. Mark felt a hot spasm in his stomach. He sat down to a table in an icy draft and clasped his hands. He looked up. Bradley stood leaning over a man at the bar, his hand on the man's shoulder.

Cathy would be sitting on his bed now, watching the dinner go cold. A new day, she had hugged him. Regular practice now, and sleep. No more nights abed looking at the ceiling. She believed he would be seated in the orchestra. His wet feet felt numb.

Bradley was sorry he had kept him waiting. Some business was too important for the office. Had he ordered? He must try a nice big juicy steak—what did he say? He was Bradley's guest, of course. Not like school days, Bradley said, looking about for other faces and smiling. They'd had a good time, though. Were women still chasing him?

"What's brandy like?" Mark asked.

"Haven't you ever had brandy?"

"I'd like a little brandy, please," Mark said to the waiter. "And coffee."

Bradley ordered the steaks bloody. "Well done for you? That's ruining it." He sat back in his chair. "But tell me about yourself. What have you been doing?"

"You work for Kellogg, do you?"

Bradley talked. He had an idea what Mark thought of places like Kellogg's Complete Creative Service. He used to think so himself in college. But let's face it: it does keep our economy going.

Mark sat turning the water glass as Bradley talked. He had caught a chill. He crossed his arms and held himself tightly. The waiter served the brandy and coffee and salad. The brandy had a revolting taste, bitter and sticky. Mark drank it all. Then he bit into a shred of lettuce, cold and tasteless like ice.

"Don't you want salad oil?"

"Thank you."

Bradley watched him. "Getting any kicks lately?"

"You should know more about kicks. Kicks and tricks."

Bradley wiped his lips. Mark had cocked his head to one side. An unpleasant smile wrung his mouth.

Bradley said, "You had a very serious ambition once, didn't you? In college?"

"Was it your ambition to work for Sylvester Kellogg?"

Bradley looked over his shoulder to see where the waiter was. "Some more brandy for you?"

"No, thank you."

Bradley leaned foward, smiling. "Say, remember the time we picketed the president's house?"

Mark rubbed his eyes. He was cold. But he did not want to see Cathy yet. She had said he would save money and move out of that miserable basement to a room above ground. A window to the sun. In time he would see how good it is to be normal, sleep nights and work days, cut his hair, squander an hour bathing, and put on a laundered shirt with cuff links. You don't know how good you look when you take care of yourself, she said.

He clawed at the salad with his fork. Bradley talked. The waiter

brought the steak, a slab of meat with small mouths oozing and bub-
bling hot blood. Mark put down his fork.

"Doesn't that look good? You can't beat this joint for steaks. I've
tried them all."

"I'm not hungry."

"Well—would you like something else? How about a nice lobster
tail?"

"No, nothing. Thank you."

The steak was very good, really, Bradley said, chewing. Wouldn't
he try just a little piece? Hate to waste a perfectly good steak, and it
would do him good. He looked underfed. He did it very well—Bradley winked—that lean look. Women went for it.

Four years had been one moment of waiting. Nothing had happened in four years. Bradley's jaw looked heavier, and he was beginning to have a belly. Mark remembered stopping at North Hall and
looking out over the empty quadrangle. Nothing was changed and
everything was gone.

"I know you never liked me," Bradley said suddenly.

"Can I have a cigarette?"

Bradley offered his pack and fumbled with his lighter. Mark lit
the cigarette with his own match.

"It used to bother me in college," Bradley said. "I thought you
were very smart, one of those people who have something on everybody. Would you like a hamburger? Another coffee?"

"Was it also your ambition to be everybody's friend?"

"I try to like everybody. I think it's a sign of maturity."

Mark felt the air conditioning on his wet feet. There was plenty of
air in this windowless cave of plastic upholstery and indirect lighting, but it was cold and stale, as in a morgue.

"How do you like Le Bistro?" Bradley asked politely.

"Fine."

Bradley laughed again, jabbing at his mutilated steak. "Excuse
me, I don't really know why I'm laughing. I guess it's your hair."

Mark disliked barbers, and let it grow. He had combed today, but
the rain had curled his hair. Cathy had pleaded with him to get a
haircut, but he had gone off to Orchestra Hall knowing he would fail

and refused a haircut out of spite. After months of erratic practice he had wanted to fail brazenly. Nobody had noticed, of course. In Le Bistro his style was out of place, but in the music hall the heads of ten of thirty cellists were overgrown, all competing for one vacancy in the city's orchestra. His disgrace was not unique, but it was delicious to toss about such a bushy crown and be dismissed after sixteen bars of the allegro. Miserable hair, and the conductor yelling "Thank you!" to stop him.

"How about some dessert?"

"No, thank you."

Bradley called for more coffee. He was in no hurry to get the reunion over with. Mark accepted another cup and another cigarette. This time Bradley did not offer his Ronson Varaflame.

"You never told me what you're doing these days. What *are* you doing these days?"

"Nothing."

"Aren't you playing?"

"Just an audition. I didn't make it."

"I'm sorry. For the Symphony Orchestra? Kind of steep, isn't it?"

"Yes."

"Any other place you can try? I mean, something with less competition?"

"No. Shall we go?"

Bradley passed a finger over the bill to verify the sum cost. Mark went to the men's room. His legs were stiff and cold. Washing his hands, he avoided the mirror. He stood undecided for a moment, his hands dripping, his face turned to the cold white tile. There were no towels in the washroom, only a machine with a nozzle that blew air, a Dri-O-Matic for his sanitary comfort. The electric wire within was shot, and the air, blown out with a whine, was icy.

Bradley drove him home in the rain. Night had come and the rain fell heavier. Streams washed over the sidewalks under the lighted lamps, and Bradley drove slowly, his eyes peering through the running windshield.

"Turn left next corner," Mark said.

The houses became squalid after a while. Small taverns appeared, then an expanse of darkness, a park, and a brick clubhouse with smashed windows. Then miles of tenement houses. They turned into a narrow street and came out on one of those obscure broad thoroughfares that are used mostly by commercial vehicles. Dirty small shops, their windows showing auto tires and used office machines, had been abandoned years ago, it seemed. They passed an old movie house, scratched and defaced; the ticket box was fashioned to resemble a clown's head, and in the grinning mouth sat an old woman nodding over a newspaper. A drugstore shone yellow in the rain, its window cluttered with dusty bottles, empty toothpaste cartons, and plastic bow ties.

Mark never left this hinterland unless he had to. The direction of life was reversed here, and he watched it with satisfaction. An oil burner set fire to a house and firemen controlled the blaze and let the house burn to the ground. A roof collapsed and a grandmother was carried out and the walls were razed. The rubble was not cleared, but patted down and left. He liked to see Blacks of a winter dawn, picks in their paws, crawling over a smoking ruin like maggots.

So there were gaps in the street past which the trucks took marvelous speed to the shining downtown. In some blocks no more than three or four houses remained. From ashes and debris sprang grass, and sometimes flowers. The city was crumbling and the prairie was coming back.

"You can always reach me at Kellogg's," Bradley said. "If you ever need anything."

"Thanks." Mark got out of the car and walked to the house in the rain.

"Don't hesitate," Bradley called.

Mark ducked down a passage between two houses and emerged in the backyard. He turned down the steps to the basement door. In the glass of the door was Cathy's face.

"You promised you'd come right home."

She was a small girl with narrow shoulders and thin arms, pretty as a child.

"The finals dragged," he said.

"You made the finals? Have they decided?"

"Next week," he lied.

"Oh, Longface!"

"No, no. There was an old cellist, some refugee. Very good. Wish you'd have heard him. Close the door."

"I bet he thinks the same of you."

They stood in the laundry room under a bare light bulb. Her brown hair touched her shoulders. She concealed her small breasts by stooping slightly. She had put on a blue wool dress. He liked her in this dress, a Peter Pan collar and satin belt. He moved to close the door.

She held him. "You see what you can do when you try! You won't knock yourself down again, will you, Longface?"

"I haven't got the job."

"Even if you don't get it, you won't lie down again. It doesn't matter, baby. You tried and I love you. If you don't make it this time, you'll make it next time. But you've got to keep trying, and I love you."

"I'm tired. Damn bus."

"Poor baby. I'll heat the dinner. Do you love me?"

"Yes, darling."

From the dark passage between the houses came the voice of Bradley Walker: "Hello!"

Bradley came in the rain carrying the cello wrong side up.

"You forgot your fiddle. God, it's like the Casbah," Bradley said, coming carefully down the steps. "You should put a light in that tunnel."

Mark introduced Bradley as an old school friend.

"I'm very pleased to meet you," Bradley said to Cathy, showing his teeth. He shook her small hand vigorously.

"Are you also a cellist?" Cathy asked.

"God, no. Kellogg's Complete Creative Service. A lot of plain hard work, that's all."

"It must be interesting work," Cathy said. She closed the door.

"*He* doesn't think so," Bradley said, smiling. "But everybody can't be a genius. Somebody has to do the dirty work and keep things going." Neither Mark nor Cathy made answer, and Bradley said, "Well, I hope we can have dinner again soon—both of you. Maybe next time he'll have a better appetite. He wouldn't touch the steak."

Cathy looked at Mark. Then she nodded to Bradley and walked out of the laundry room into the basement.

Bradley looked around. "Wonderful tubs. My mother wore herself to death over a sink like that. You don't live here?"

"My room's up front."

Mark turned to the window. The glass was dirty and he could not see through. It was raining hard and steady.

Bradley tried to see where Cathy had disappeared. Beyond the laundry room the basement fell into darkness. Wash lines were strung within, heavy with wet sheets, and the air smelled humid and sour.

"Brad, would you mind taking her home? The bus runs only on the hour."

Bradley said, "Glad to. Where does she live?"

"Elmview. Can you wait a second? . . . No, come in."

Mark took the cello and slipped in ahead. Bradley followed slowly. They bent low to clear the wash lines, ducked between sheets, and stepped around ashcans. At the boiler Mark halted and listened. They moved on past a row of stalls in which tenants kept their rubbish under lock. A light showed in the cracks of a partition at the far end, next to a coal bin. Mark opened a small door and they went in.

Cathy sat on a narrow steel bed. She had pulled a blanket over her shoulders and held the ends in her small fists. A pot of coffee steamed on a two-burner gas range, a bridge table was laid prettily for two. The glasses sparkled. A line of books and some stacks of music were arranged neatly on a large desk under the window. Tacked to the wall was a print cut from a magazine. The sound of rain beat on the window.

"Cathy," Mark said. He stood the cello in its corner and sat beside her.

The girl showed no surprise at seeing Bradley again. Her eyes turned to the window and there they held.

Mark reached for her hand, but she pulled it away. "Later," he said. "Brad will take you home now."

Bradley fidgeted with his car keys. Mark fetched her coat. As he held the coat for her she let go of the blanket and rose on unsteady feet. He brought her handbag and white gloves.

"Lucky thing, Brad driving you home. You won't need your boots after all. But wear them next time."

"My car's double-parked," Bradley said. "I hope it's all right."

"They don't bother you here."

Cathy ran out of the room. She knocked into something, and ran on. The yard door opened and she was out.

Mark opened the window. As Cathy passed on the sidewalk he called her name. She did not stop.

He closed the window and stood listening to the rain. A kitchen clock on the dresser showed twenty minutes past nine. The bus would not come for forty minutes.

"Nothing, don't worry," Mark said. "She'll be standing three blocks down, where the bus stops. Will you pick her up there? I'll appreciate it."

Bradley stood looking at him.

Mark tossed his hand. "She may not want to come at first. Will you do that?"

"Aren't you coming?"

"No."

Bradley left.

Mark uncased the cello and began to dry it with a rag. The cello was not wet, only its back was damp. He rubbed it all over, and said aloud to himself, "Won't be in a hurry this year."

In Line for Lemonade

Alexander Pashkov, a dixie cup in his hand, was moving with the line toward the lemonade bowl in the Young People's Lounge. He had the round face of a tired child, a stubby nose and large dark eyes; on his head was a fine mass of black hair which he never managed to part twice in the same place, so that in spite of careful combing he looked unkempt.

He pretended to some knowledge of Moscow, where he was born forty years before, but never mentioned his having been taken to Germany at the age of three, where he grew up. Most of his adult years were spent knocking about among refugees and intellectual flotsam. He studied in Berlin and then in Zurich, where he wrung out a book on the literature of German expatriates. Just before the war he floundered into Paris on his way to America.

There were flocks of homeless birds in those days who knew wars in the offing and knew whither to fly. Pashkov was one of them. He came to America and sat out the war and was taken on by Midwestern College. He had at once felt at home in America. Americans are really a homeless people, he reflected, even the wealthy ones. They have a big continent and automobiles. He liked Maplewood as he might have liked a comfortable inn, the trees, the college, and the fashionable Methodist church, a two-million-dollar edifice in which it was a pleasure to make a harmless confession of faith.

In his youth Alexander Pashkov had wanted to become a poet. The ambition in the adolescent grew to shame in the man. He had lived his poetic ambition so intensely, had crowded his wandering years with so much dreaming and so little doing, that now, being settled and nearing forty, he had found it hard to let the poet in him die. He had tried to work, God knows, but nothing came of it. He wrote best in Russian and German, but he had never decided which was *his* language. His good judgment smiled at him in his German attempts and roared at him in the Russian, and so he flung himself back and forth like a madman between two mirrors.

And yet the day came when his poetic ambition died, and it died without pain. It was mercifully killed by honor from an unexpected quarter. A routine academic essay of his on Mayakovsky, appearing in a literary quarterly on the twentieth anniversary of the poet's suicide, attracted attention. Pashkov had a restrained English prose and his fragments of translation from Mayakovsky came off happily. The editor of the periodical flattered himself on having uncovered a new talent.

Pashkov was invited to contribute something more on Soviet literature. He knew the tides of fashion and replied with an appreciation of Yesenin. Although he scarcely knew Yesenin and had in fact come too late to this poet to translate him with sympathy, he received a number of letters from scholars in the land, solicitations from two obscure magazines, and an inquiry from a New York publisher who smelled a market.

At bottom he mistrusted his talent. He stuck to his first editor with a long paper on the Soviet Futurists. He steered clear of Communist ideology so as not to clutter his literary criticism with political comment. Instead of unmasking his slippery hold of the subject, his timidity was praised in Letters to the Editor as "masterful detachment," and a student in California wrote in that Pashkov's approach was "the very thing America needs at a time when mad reactionary dogs are running loose in Washington."

Pashkov was in despair. His interest was literary, he disliked and feared politics, and his only wish was to pass unnoticed by the nests of vipers he saw stirring about him. To make matters worse, he could not help cheating a little in his essays, could not resist making small references here and there to poets and schools and "influences" of which he knew nothing. Nobody, he realized gloomily, not even the chairman of his department at Midwestern, saw through his ignorance. That piece on the Futurists had been a risky job. He would be more careful.

He had the good fortune at this time to meet Thomas Eisner, the great translator of Russian classics, who came to Midwestern for two days. At the lecture-tea Eisner took Pashkov aside.

"I have read some of your work," the famous personage said in beautiful Russian. "You are not a critic, dear Mr. Pashkov. You are a poet, somewhat like the English Fitzgerald."

Pashkov stared, and the ponderous Eisner smiled down at him and nodded and said, "Yes."

Pashkov wanted to weep, as though his sins had rolled away. Was he to be a poet after all?

He wanted to thank Eisner, but the oracle was too much for him. He pressed Eisner's hand and blushed. He came home in high spirits.

He set to work. A "translator" of poetry? he mused with a smile, working on Blok. For the first time since his youth he felt that he was growing. When he came to Pasternak he was jubilant. He had found himself. He was a sort of Fitzgerald, he reminded himself, and a sort of Conrad who would not have written at all if not in English. As the year passed he became a small name to people who knew what was happening in the world.

He was touched by a desire he had not known. He got the notion of topping his happiness with a pleasant marriage. His success was after all too one-sided, too public, too much like a display that does not satisfy the performer deeply. There would always be work for him, he might even achieve a small place—but he dared think no further. He thought instead of a wife who would fill the vacancy in him.

There was a vacancy in him. He admitted it. Something in him had not been engaged in his work, a part of him had not bitten into Eisner's flattering words, had remained untouched, unexercised, left to rot in his soul, to petrify, to create darkness and frighten him. Alexander Pashkov needed a wife.

For a man who had traveled so much his lovelife was disappointing. There had been women. In the closing days before the war, Paris was enlivened by numerous cross-currents of festive people meeting and parting for the last time. There was dancing and music. He remembered the poet Tagkvist with his fake anecdotes about Lagerlof and Hedin and even Hamsun, his shrill voice above a crowd offering him his mistress for a week. Very drunk for a Swede. Tagkvist ran ahead introducing Pashkov as the celebrated author of *Hesse and Others*, which nobody had read, a cheap paperback edition that lay forgotten in the basement of a publisher nobody had heard of. Tagkvist had fashioned this fact into an acceptable calling card for Pashkov. Goodness knows who all was there, in one or another of the whooping holes the Swede dragged him to. Names and self-made names, and always some repulsive Bebert in the company of nonchalant Americans.

Pashkov might have had something to remember had he not disappointed the women. His Napoleonic height was no impediment, they liked him the more for his child's stature and fondled him with the sharp sensuality that makes the corruption of innocents such a pleasure. In bed his small figure, his unkempt hair and big dark eyes made him look like a little boy. But Pashkov allowed the women little fun. He could not help it. He got carried away, he trembled into oblivion and immediately fell to sleep.

Well, he was not a lover. Worse, he had never loved. It was as if his love had been stopped in childhood by some horrid and commonplace experience, and hid itself at every appeal to the man. There was a big girl from Cherbourg who fell in love with him. Pashkov fled to other arms. Not without melancholy. Why couldn't he love?

If truth must be told, he did not even love his work. He was making an Anthology now. His publisher insisted on something "comprehensive." He would have to include a lot of facetious muck written by order of the Politburo. There were moments of pleasure when a good poem came his way, but he had lost his freedom in the publisher's contract. And Midwestern College expected a "major production." He sent off the manuscript and started to look for a woman he might marry.

How pretty the women here were, how perfectly they dressed. But how unapproachable. A riddle, their infinite care of appearance and icy chastity. Sunday morning he watched them walking under the shade trees, swinging their hips to church, dressed and painted like the more expensive Parisian whores, not too gaudily, not too modestly. They were afraid of something, he thought with satisfaction—afraid of discoloration, of poverty. It was a good fear, it was what attracted Pashkov.

Forty years old. Yes, it was time to settle down. The college humor magazine, *Banana*, had four pages caricaturing members of the faculty. "Guess Who?" There were storks wearing pince-nez, hippopotamuses, gazelles, lions and crows. On the bars in the gymnasium swung a couple of apes, from the English Department emerged a mild-eyed horse. Pashkov found himself and was not displeased. On the Slavonic branch of the Tree of Languages sat a harmless little lemur. The caption read: "One of our lemures?"

He did not know whether *Banana* knew the difference between lemurs and lemures, between the arboreal mammals and the souls of the dead.

One day a religious worker knocked on his door with solicitations for a settlement in the slums. Pashkov gave generously and two months later the same mendicant returned with an appeal for the underfed in Malaya and an invitation to "meet the folks" at the church. A nice quiet woman, flashed through his mind. He had explored the local movie houses and parks, timidly and with a wary eye. The social life of the town was gruesome—in fact, it did not seem to exist. Possibly in the church? Why had he not thought of the church before?

But he had to go to New York just then. The appearance of his Anthology made it necessary for him to attend an autographing party. He put off thinking about a nice quiet woman.

In New York a junior editor showed him the town. The Anthology was selling well enough. Reviews ranged from talk about two great peoples exchanging ideas to the wisdom of knowing one's enemy. Pashkov knew the book was worthless.

"Doesn't Thomas Eisner live in New York?" Pashkov asked his guide.

"Long Island. Would you like to meet him?"

"No, no. I was just wondering. I could not find him in the telephone directory."

"He'd hardly be listed," the young man said. He gave Pashkov a thin smile. "I have his address in my desk. I'd be glad to introduce you."

Eisner had turned down Pashkov's request for a review of his book.

On the morning of his last day in New York Pashkov traveled to Long Island. The house was rather small; it stood on a large lawn; about the house stood a scattering of slender birch trees.

A Black housemaid took his name in, came back and ushered him into a large bedroom, where the man sat behind a breakfast tray.

"So good of you to call on me," Eisner said. He offered his hand. "I have a cold."

That beautiful Russian language, Pashkov thought, and felt a vague longing. But he scarcely touched his hand.

"Mary, bring us a chair. Will you have tea, Mr. Pashkov?"

"Thank you, no." He sat on the edge of the chair and leaned forward, clasping his hands.

"No doubt you wonder why I could not review your Anthology," Eisner said.

Pashkov raised a protesting hand, dropped it and wrung his fingers.

"I did look at it. Very nice. But I am terribly busy just now. It appears we live in an age of deadlines. Is it selling well?"

Pashkov nodded.

"You've got to be careful here. Don't let them cheat you. Who is your agent?"

"I have no agent, Mr. Eisner."

"But that's not good. Shall I introduce you to my Zhivchick? Fine business sense. What have you next in mind? What are you working on now?"

Pashkov looked down at his hands. They were moist.

"I have been thinking of Khlebnikov," he said in a small, subdued voice.

"Hm."

"Not so much Khlebnikov's work," Pashkov's voice rose. "I was thinking of his life, his travels."

"What, a biography?"

"Well, not exactly. The typhoid, the army in Persia. A man . . . a poem, in fact, but a biographical, that is, panoramic. . . ."

Pashkov opened his mouth for air.

"What?"

"After your lecture in Midwestern, if you remember. You said—" He covered his face. "You said I was a poet."

Pashkov waited, but Eisner remained silent.

At last he looked up. Eisner was stirring his tea.

"I've said a great many things, Mr. Pashkov. But one book is nothing to get upset about. We are too impatient with ourselves."

"What shall I do?"

"Work."

"Mr. Eisner," Pashkov said. "Mr. Eisner," he repeated, "is there any hope?"

Eisner hesitated a moment. "You're asking an impossible question," he said. "And after all, what else is there to do?"

Just then Mary knocked on the door. Eisner waved her out but Pashkov had already taken up his coat.

He smiled. "Strange, isn't it, Mr. Eisner, that some people need to be told they are worth something, and others that they are worth nothing."

"I am not sure I understand."

"Perhaps there's nothing to understand."

And so Alexander Pashkov went back to Maplewood with the thought that he must find a woman, a woman not to be distinguished from the smooth cement of those tidy streets, one of the lacquered beauties. To lose himself. And where better than in a two-million-dollar church?

Pashkov went to the Sunday morning service. He had time now, he would explore his adopted country, find his little hole and drop in. He sat in a padded pew somewhat to the side, toward the rear, on the edge of well-dressed worship.

Thereafter he was seen regularly at the Sunday afternoon social in the Young People's Lounge. He was always very polite and everybody liked him.

Americans are quite right, thought Pashkov. They lead the nations, they have the wisdom of babes. They are right for me, he smiled. He did not know whether they were right for themselves. That did not concern him, that was another question.

He held the dixie cup and moved with the line toward the lemonade bowl.

Afternoon of a Sleepwalker

His son was three years old when Janine divorced him. She remarried a week later. On Ben's last day with her, in the evening, he took Joey to the park playground and watched him play in the sandbox. After a while he noticed it was getting dark. The boy was bringing sand pies, smiling up at him sideways the way Janine smiled. Ben thanked him for every pie, and Joey climbed back into the box to bake another as the moon was rising.

Janine did not scold him for coming back so late. She gave him a glass of pineapple juice, and he took it to the bedroom and watched his son tilting the glass with both hands, gulping the juice. Then Ben covered him up and kissed him and turned out the light. Joey stretched up his arms and said, "Kiss!"

"Go to sleep," Ben said, standing by the bed in the dark room. He bent down and kissed him on the mouth. Then he crossed to the door, but his hand would not reach for the knob. He stood there, his back to the bed. The boy kicked off the blanket and began to talk to himself.

Going out, Ben closed the bedroom door softly. Janine sat hunched up on the couch. She was sobbing. He got his coat and went to her. She looked at him sideways. Her hair was mussed. As he kissed her on the head, she brought her face to his shoulder and held him. Then he got up and left the apartment, and that was how their marriage ended.

Janine and Joey went to Los Angeles to live where her new husband, Robert, had a future in plastics engineering. Ben did not often think about Joey. He sent him a glossy picture book for Christmas, and a big chocolate egg for Easter. The chocolate egg melted on the way, so all his son got was the greeting card. Janine wrote letters and signed them with Joey's name and much love. Ben wrote back and said that was fine. He had quit his job in the shoe store on Ninth Avenue, next to a dancing studio, and lived carefully on his savings. He read Janine's letters and put them away, and walked in Central Park.

Joey's fourth birthday party was a long letter. Two snapshots. He put away the snapshots and the long letter, and went out to celebrate. He came back to his room quite late, on very steady feet, and lay down and slept.

And then summer came and he went out to Long Island to see Anita de Lamadrid, who still went by the name of Ann Carlton, on Ninth Avenue. Anita looked sleepy and said what the hell, and she talked about opening her own dancing studio on Long Island. Ben said she would be a big success, and wished her lots of luck.

He sat in his room, reading magazines and Janine's letters. He tried to get up at the same time every morning, and when he overslept he made himself do things he did not like to do—polish his shoes, or write a postcard to his uncle.

When Janine wrote that Robert wanted to adopt his son, Ben wrote back asking if that was necessary. Janine said it was. She said it would be a clean break, it would be easier on Joey when he started school, and it would make Robert and her very happy. Ben said he would be willing to settle for anything short of adoption. Janine said after denying his son the companionship of a real father, never worrying about him from the day he was born, with no more interest in Joey than in a plaything, was he now trying to have his rights? She was sorry if it hurt, but the fact was his son had found a real father in Robert, who had a good future because he worked hard. Every morning Joey and Robert brushed their teeth together, and every evening the boy ran to the window to look for Robert.

Ben called up Mr. Rosen and made an appointment.

"You ought to let them have him," Mr. Rosen said. "He will

understand when he grows up."

"Is there no other way?"

"It's the best thing for all concerned," Mr. Rosen said. "Unless you have definitely made up your mind not to let them adopt him. Have you?"

"I want him to be happy."

"That's right," Mr. Rosen said.

"I don't want him to think his daddy didn't love him."

"He won't think that. They understand when they grow up."

The phone rang. Ben looked at the brown leather buttons in Mr. Rosen's brown leather chair.

Mr. Rosen put down the receiver. "You bring me the form she sends. I'll go across the street with you and have it registered."

"I lose all rights to my son?" he asked. "Visiting rights?"

"Legally, you lose all rights. But only legally. They won't stand in your way, will they?"

"I don't think so."

"You do that," Mr. Rosen said, fingering a slender cigarette lighter. It resembled Ben's own wind-proof lighter, except that his was thicker and inscribed from Janine.

"All right," he said.

Ben wrote to Janine to send the adoption papers, and he would sign them. His window stood open to the summer evening. He mailed the letter, and went out to Long Island to see Anita.

Anita looked sleepy and said what the hell, and she talked about opening her own dancing studio on Long Island. He said she would be a big success. Anita was getting heavier, he noticed, as she came from the bedroom wearing tight jeans. She made the drinks on the coffee table.

"Don't you notice anything different?" she asked him.

"What?"

"I redecorated!"

"Looks very nice, Anita."

"How do you like this?" she said, standing before a bullfight poster, sipping from her glass.

"That's nice," he said. "That's real nice."

They sat on Anita's convertible davenport. A breeze came in at the window, a smell of the sea.

"You spoil it drinking so fast. That's all I have is that bottle."

"I'll get another," he offered.

"No."

"Just take a minute. I'll be right back."

"What's the matter with you?" she said. "Can't you sit still?"

He sat looking at his drink.

"I don't like it the way you come here," Anita said. "I never did like it, once in a blue moon when you have nothing better to do." She made another drink. "What do you hear from your wife? Your ex-wife."

"Cut it out."

Anita set the drink before him, took his head in her arms, and combed his hair with her fingers. "Why can't you be good to me?" she said. "Like you used to."

"I don't mean to be mean."

"You never change," Anita said, pushing him away. "I get so bored," she said, staring at her bullfight poster. "Jesus, I get so bored."

"What are you bored about?"

"I get scared sometimes," Anita said. "Why can't you be good to me, baby?"

He went out to the corner drug and liquor store and bought another bottle, but when he came back Anita would not open the door. He waited a long time, maybe five minutes. Then he left the bottle by the door and went home.

He slept late into the next day, past noon, and when he got up he saw it had been a nice day and it was mostly gone. He went out and took his late breakfast in a restaurant he could not afford. Juice of mixed fruit, poached eggs on muffins, marmalade, Dutch coffee.

A fine afternoon for a walk. On his way to the park he passed the horse cabs that stood in line as in a picture postcard. A ride in a horse cab might have been fun once, and afterwards a sidewalk cafe. Such good weather lately, so many perfect summer days! A cool breeze touched his face.

He saw them from afar, a woman and a small boy, there on a bench among the trees. He crossed the lawn to the path that would take him past them. They had not chosen the pond where the tin rowboats steered for floating dixie cups, oars squeaking in the oarlocks; they had removed themselves to a bench among the trees, the woman in summer pastels, a broad yellow hat flowered with blue, its rim taking the sun this summer afternoon.

He walked along the path trying not to stare. The boy was four or five years old, he could see now, a blue suit with brass buttons, short pants, and white shoes. The boy had found a stone and was showing it to the woman, leaning over her knees, and they were discussing. Ben walked toward them on the path.

But he had to stop to light a cigarette. His wind-proof lighter always worked, inscribed from Janine, though in the open it was best to shelter the flame with his hand. Shelter the flame. His lungs took in the smoke, and he did not look at the woman and the child. He would simply walk by.

"Hello," said the child as he passed. A grown-up hello, but a sound from a time when words have more music than meaning.

"Well, hello there," he said, without seeing the child, unable for a moment to direct his eyes, seeing instead the woman's shoes, their heels slender but not too high. He looked up at her face, as if to ask permission. She was smiling a little, holding her head to one side, but not offering acquaintance.

"Hello," the boy said again.

"Hello again," he said.

The boy was radiant, beautiful, standing on a carpet of dappled sun and leaves, scattering his musical hellos.

"Charles," the woman said. It was not a reprimand, only a reminder, and the boy gave him the path, backed off to the woman's extended hand, giving his face a secret twitch.

The woman inclined her head, it was scarcely a nod, not enough to invite conversation, and he could not stop, but continued on his way. It was not long, then, one minute, two, before he turned with the path, walking not too fast.

And for the second time that day Ben spent more money than he should have—for a ride in a horse cab.

As he settled back in the hard leather, the vehicle seemed enormous to him. A party of three could ride in it comfortably. He edged himself into the corner, crossed his legs, and sank back. The sky was blue. The sun would be good for another two hours, he thought.

The horse's hoofs click-clacked, the wheels turned, and the carriage swayed, cradling the vague pleasure he felt. Janine had left him something gentle, he thought—like a sleep in a hammock on a summer afternoon.

Shadows on the Water

I

My brother died a suicide in Newhall Hospital, California. He was forty-nine, seven years my senior. At sundown, as I carried his phonograph and a cardboard box of his effects to the parking lot, a man detached himself from a group of inmates on the lawn and joined me. His name was Robert Sladick, but everybody at Newhall called him Doc. Before his commitment Mr. Sladick had taught philosophy at the California State College at Morley. Talkative as a janitor, helpful and kind, he ran errands for the nurses, expressed opinions about books, and had perhaps spent more time with my brother than anybody else at Newhall.

"I see you got Tom's stuff," he said. "How are you feeling?"

"Fine. How are you, Mr. Sladick?"

"Here, let me help you." He took the phonograph. It was a cheap portable model intended for the teenage market, its case decorated with red white and blue stripes, its cover picturing a dancing girl in a bikini. Tom had bought the phonograph when he went to the hospital. Mr. Sladick peered in the cardboard box. "You got his records?" he asked.

"I got them." The cardboard box contained books, mostly, and three phonograph recordings: Nazi marching songs, Red Army songs, and gospel songs.

"All Tom cared about was this Carlyle book and the Nazi

songs," said Mr. Sladick, trudging along beside me. "I'm getting a pass for his funeral."

I thanked him. Tom had hardly known anybody the last few years.

"They say he did it with Veronal?" asked Mr. Sladick.

"That's right."

"I'm really sorry," he said. "I wish he could have waited a year. Reforms take time. In a year, Tom might have been active again."

"Doing what?"

"He could have been a professor of mystical literature."

We passed two ambulances at Emergency. The parking lot ended at a high wire fence. A guard sat in the guardhouse by the gates.

"If you want to bury yourself," said Mr. Sladick, "bury your talents. That's what Tom did. He had it all at his fingertips—demons, devils, witches. But he did nothing with it."

"He was a priest for a while," I said.

"No, he wasn't," said Mr. Sladick. "Your father was a real Russian priest, trained and ordained. Tom's license from that crazy outfit didn't make him anything."

The cardboard box felt heavy in my arms. Except for a fitful nap on the 727, I had not slept since leaving Boston. I wanted my bed at the Sheraton Arms in Hollywood. I put the cardboard box and the phonograph in the Hertz car and got in behind the wheel.

"Look," said Mr. Sladick, "why don't you come see me tomorrow? I know a lot about Tom. How about lunch? I'll give you a good debriefing."

I had to bury Tom, settle matters with our lawyer, and fly back to Boston. "I'm fine, Doc. Thanks just the same."

"You don't look fine. Is that hill in Los Feliz all yours now?"

"Yes."

"Get rid of it," he said. "Tom figured you could get $250,000 for it. Somebody wants to build a posh dining place up there."

"They'd have to tear down the church."

"I know all about that church," said Mr. Sladick. "Give it to

Disneyland. That's what Tom would have done, next time
around."

"I have to go now, Mr. Sladick. Thanks for the talk. I appreciate it."

"Wait a minute," he said. He walked around the car and got in
beside me.

I should have locked the door. The guard, I saw, sat in the
guardhouse, watching us.

Mr. Sladick said, "You have a brother who killed himself, and
you have the same blood. I should think you'd want to know why
he killed himself."

"Why did he kill himself?"

"I don't know. I'm only saying you'll want to think about it.
While you're at it, think about Los Angeles. You know how Tom
hated Los Angeles. I understand you can see much of Los Angeles
from that hill of yours?"

"Mr. Sladick, I've got to get some sleep. I'll call you tomorrow,
if I can. I'll know then what my schedule will be. All right?"

"You won't call," he said. "Let me tell you something, as long
as you're here. People live in Los Angeles. How do you think they
get by? They are adjusted to little systems like the I-Thou Temple
or The Church of the Open Door, or The First Church of the
Divine Mushroom. And not just churches. Neighborhood clubs,
VFW posts, local taverns, political parties, motorcycle gangs,
marriages. I was telling Tom last week: suppose you made a cata-
log of these institutions and listed their members, who would
not be accounted for? Even the bum on his last leg has his daily
haunts. All part of Los Angeles. And Los Angeles is part of
America, and America is part of the world, and the world is part
of the galaxies. Do you know what keeps this house of cards from
coming down?"

I didn't.

"We bang around enough in it to bring it down," he said.
"When your father died Tom could play with that cute church
and invent his own religion, if I can believe him. He loved metaphysical panic. But when your mother died he had no system left,

just himself."

"Did he ever talk about me?"

"He didn't need you," said Mr. Sladick. "He had his Carlyle and his Nazis."

The sun had set and gusts blew sand over the parking lot.

"What about you, now?" said Mr. Sladick. "Are you still teaching Russian in Boston?"

"Yes."

"Crummy job. Professors have to write books nobody wants to write and nobody wants to read."

"That's true."

"All right, but don't quit. What would your next institution be? Do you know what Tom's last institution was, when his goofy religion folded? The Piggery on La Cienega."

The Piggery, an architectural fantasy squeezed in between The Tahitian Hut and The Roaring Twenties on La Cienega Boulevard's Restaurant Row, was built to resemble a pig with a pork chop in its mouth. It was a dark hangout for young people, bodies writhing to deafening rock, pinball machines, shrieks. At the exit in the rear, you stepped on a rubber mat that activated an electronic fart. Tom had been attracted for a season to noisy amusements. He visited roller coasters and tilt-a-whirls, and reported that the pleasures of youth are the torments of age.

"Tom used to eat hamburgers there," said Mr. Sladick. "He'd pick up girls at the I-Thou Temple just to take them to The Piggery. That was his last institution."

I closed my eyes for a moment, and when I opened them the lights atop the hospital fence were lit. I could not decide whether the lights were functional or decorative.

"That's what happened to me, in a way," said Mr. Sladick. "You must know the risk of losing your wits if you step outside the institution. It's mad enough inside."

One day, Mr. Sladick went on to relate, when he was teaching at Morley College, he walked into his classroom and saw himself, or thought he saw himself, writing incomprehensible cryptography on the blackboard. To his amazement the students seemed familiar with it: they copied, read, discussed. Mr. Sladick stood at the lectern paralyzed, but another self within him held forth. Thereafter, he was habitually inspired in class and absentminded out of class. He had always cultivated dullness to save energy and sighed gratefully when the cretins avoided him, but that year he got the Distinguished Teacher's Award and was elected chairman of the Philosophy Department's Long-Range Planning Committee. Beside himself, he sensed mortal danger. At the award party he caught himself making indecent proposals to the dean's wife. He also flattered a colleague for publishing an unreadable book. Appalled, he quit teaching in a reckless moment of self-confidence. "And here I am."

Mr. Sladick got out of the car. "See you at the funeral," he said. "You'd better get some sleep. You look terrible."

I drove to Los Angeles. Gently rocking on the freeway at night, the lights of small towns passed on the right or on the left. In my somnolence I could feel, as did schoolmen of the Middle Ages, that time is an illusion and we exist in an abiding present. *"Alle Menschen müssen sterben,"* sings Bach. All people must die. The day before, I had been reading an encyclopedic punster sparkling with transitive verbs (a sign of genius) who recommended total rejection of all religions ever dreamt up by man and total composure in the face of total death. If we knew why people lose their heads, total composure would be totally admirable. But I did not know why my brother lost his head, and why I might keep or lose mine.

After dinner once at the home of a backsliding Unitarian, Tom and I argued into the small hours whether our hunger was moral or aesthetic. Believer and unbeliever, Tom and I went at it with some heat, perversely lighting the way for each other. Tom explained why women tempted him. When he understood himself best, he said, the devil tempted him most. The devil had reason to tempt, considering the prize, and over the years the devil had increased the temptations in pitch and frequency until Tom found his happiness on the threshold to the Nothing of All, and expected an illumination. Doubts? "The more I doubt, the more I believe," said Tom. What with the wine and the Unitarian's sloppy grinning—"That's the divine *nihil*, right?"—the mystery deepened and we began to lose our threads. Then our host's five-year-old daughter entered the room clad in Snoopy pajamas. She had been awakened by our shouts and derisive laughter, and came to kiss us all good-night. Which she did. Who made the little lamb? I wondered, hoping she would blow away our verbal smoke with an angelic utterance. It was not to be. If God spoke through the child, He spoke only through her warm cheek on mine. But I did not trust my intention to read a message, or God's to send one. Truth is the death of intention, I have seen, and the mere consciousness of belief corrupts the affirmation. Please send me useless things.

II

In his youth my father had been a monk at the Zagorsk monastery near Moscow. He had knelt with other monks around fourteenth-century manuscripts, sung responses, blest the candles, cleaned the ikons, shed tears over the corpse of his Elder. He had lain prostrate on icy flagstones for his sins, swept paths in the snow with a twig broom, sat in the chapel vestibule with cripples and widows, gossiping and chewing his ration of sausage and dill pickle. He had kissed three corners of a golden reliquary as priest and choir winged their spirits into ancient beliefs.

For some years after the Revolution he served as Auxiliary of the Patriarch of Riga. In those days we dressed for dinner, my mother in flowing green with a high lace collar, my father in a fresh cassock smelling of soap and winter air, I still in my Fauntleroy, and Tom in his first long pants and tie, his buttocks on the chair mashing his student cap for rakish effect, putting the ceremony of dinner to some use.

The sun flooding the dining room tinted one and another crystal pendant in the chandelier, and in the shadowed corner glowed the grandfather clock, its face composing the spheres of sun and moon, the stars and all the planets in inlaid mother-of-pearl. Beside the clock arched a Romanesque window with a border of stylized flowers in stained glass, red roses and white lilies, eternally stiff and fresh. The white lace curtains tied with yellow tasseled cords formed a theatrical curtain for the show in the window. Slow taxis and droshkies in the wintry street, the frozen canal winding through the park past the Opera white with snow. Afar behind a line of trees stretched the parade grounds. A clear freezing day for military exercises. Companies of brown horses bearing uniformed riders, and one white horse, pranced and galloped toylike, pennants fluttering and trumpets flashing in the sun.

When the finger-bowls of perfumed water were served, my father opened the gilded Scripture and saw reflected in his memory of Zagorsk, as in a mirror, Isaiah's Zion, city of solemnities. This City, he would read to my fidgeting brother and me, is a quiet habitation, a tabernacle that shall not be taken down; not one of the stakes thereof shall ever be removed, neither shall any of the cords thereof be broken. "For here we have no continuing city, but we seek one to come."

In the Byzantine Cathedral on holy days, I would see him in gold and lace, a smoking censer in his hand, his pectoral cross set with rubies. I held my breath when he bowed low to the great altar and the martyrs in heaven. Row on row the painted saints stood ranged in proper order, above and below, long bodies and small heads, their faces showing neither joy nor sorrow as they witnessed the Terrible Judgment in the vast fresco over the main portals. Christ, enthroned, seemed indifferent to the snake writhing up from torture chambers, where sinners, their faces also expressionless, were speared, quartered, and eaten by demons, in truth and justice.

In our world we preferred art to science. We would have been dismayed, when coming upon an astonishing circle of mushrooms in the forest, to learn that they marked the periphery of underground mycelial growth. Give us the work of mild terror and joy, a ring of dancing fairies, such as eventually blossomed in Tom's familiarity with the devil, his taste, as Mr. Sladick had put it, for metaphysical panic. A streak in the family. And all it needed to go haywire was a Southern California free of the past and the future.

After the loss of Zagorsk and the loss of Riga, their ancient stakes removed and their cords broken, my father promptly restored the promise to himself by building his own little Zagorsk in California, which he called Old Russia, on a forty-acre hilltop in Los Feliz with a grand view of Los Angeles. A priest's house, a quaint little Russian church of plaster and paint, and a graveyard. In Southern California nothing seemed more natural than a gilded Russian church between a ghostly Taj Mahal and a coy Swiss chalet on adjoining hills. And behold, wonder of the country, film companies offered money for location work, and when the first film crew clattered into our garden with cables and reflectors, he realized that he had succeeded and failed.

His brain could not comprehend the distance he had traveled from Zagorsk to Hollywood. "Beware the chains of gold!" But who could resist money in 1932, 1933, 1934, the country crashing and people running to the movies, my mother learning to peel potatoes and not touch the vacuum cleaner during rare thunderstorms. "What a wild country!" she said happily, digging a hole by the path to the church, to plant a lemon tree, while my father sat on a bench nearby, reading a journal from Berlin.

In time everything he built collasped, and my brother could thank him for his interest in the devil. Everybody knows something about the devil, but those who are puzzled by their successes and failures can sometimes recognize the shapes he assumes. His works are many. Consider the spells he casts, the dreams he sends, the vanities he insinuates, the illusions he spins, the victories he grants, the defeats he disguises, the prayers he teaches, the talents he strengthens, and the manner of his teasing and tormenting and delighting body and soul, as he walks about seeking whom he may devour.

Father and mother dead, I removed myself as far as I could, to Boston's stone houses and real gutters.

My brother alone remained to play with the church he inherited, the vestments, the jewelry and holy pictures, licensed to his own notion of the priesthood by the I-Thou Temple in Hollywood.

III

For some years Tom rode the heady currents of spiritual fashion, mingling with truth-finders on inexpressible mental trips. He opened his doors to emissaries of maharishis, perfect masters, God, and the Mushroom, one slack-jawed anarchist bringing glad tidings of the atomic holocaust, and ate rice and sat with them in a circle on the floor of the church, holding hands for fellowship and purification.

The Balaban & Katz theater chairs that he had installed for an earlier wave of existentialists were pushed to the walls to make room for religious body language, Christ present now in new contexts, drums and electric guitars. Resplendent in our father's priestly robes and jewels, he intoned from the Secret Gospel According to Mark the sweet news that Jesus was a bi-sexual troilist. And one fine night during the expressive dance-testimony of a sixty-two-year-old stripper wearing a purple wig, naked to offer her dugs humbly to the Lord, her last mite, two scouts from the Hell's Angels roared up to check out the I-Thou Russian Church, having heard good things. They came to scoff and stayed to cavort, their iron crosses and swastikas inspiring Tom to sing a Wehrmacht song, German words, for which they swore their love, kissed him, promised to castrate all who did him bodily harm, and thundered off whooping and hollering through the graveyard and a neighbor's putting green, their exploding bikes plowing the grave mounds and chewing up the nice turf.

All this was correct, Tom said to me when I visited him after his second nervous breakdown. He was by then a gaunt recluse in Old Russia, shambling to our graveyard in slippers and a tattered robe, to pay respects to Father and Mother in their graves. It was correct to sniff the rank creative pit between the death of one religion and the birth of another worthy of the name. Everything was going back to the great steaming pit, he said, the gurus and the messengers, the astrologers and calcified Christians, the oblivious youth worshipping the kingdom within—all bubbles in the ooze, and the fun may simmer a thousand years before another shape emerges true as Byzantium. For his part, boredom had set in. And fear.

He had found a little waitress near UCLA, a Peggy who resented working nights until two, serving drinks, getting goosed, sick of people making off with her tips. In a Howard Johnson's motel (free TV) he did the act of darkness with her and loved to hear her talk: "Sometimes you can really acquire a warped perspective of people, being a waitress? Catering to the public? Most of them are college students, only enough money to pay for drinks. You begin to look at people only how they are going to benefit you. Like, a source of income, not personalities with something more valuable. Kissing ass for a lousy dime is a rotten thing to have to do." Peggy could have done ITT measurable good, and Tom had listened to her with the interest he would have accorded a talking cat.

Nothing came of it, thank God. The church padlocked now and the graveyard and garden gone to weeds, Tom remained alone in the priest's house, ignoring creditors and studying ways to purge himself of a madness inflicted by girls in short dresses. He found women to be nymphs, monsters, demons in the classical dictionaries of Lemprière, Quicherat, and Grimal, and debated whether to commit himself to Newhall.

The place was expensive but comfortably appointed, and the service, he had heard from a connoisseur, matched that of a European hotel of the old school. Go back a bit, if you can't go forward a thousand years. A little custom and ceremony. Here in Old Russia he had relieved himself utterly of social duties. The house needed repairs and was going to hell. He had neglected to hire a gardener to mow the lawns and prune the bushes. The sight of the neighbor's gardener stepping on slimy snails moved him to tears of boredom. He needed an asylum to structure his days and concentrate his recalcitrant intelligence.

"Well, if you think . . ." I said tentatively, careful not to discourage him with my approval.

On the other hand, he said, he could not ignore the advantages of remaining in Old Russia to pursue his investigations.

I thought: a poor little waitress with a cute ass. Tom the Hippie courting spiritual suffering. *Difficult is the descent to God.* As he speculated, I could see in the window, stretching away to the horizon, the lights of Los Angeles beginning to glimmer, steaming with the luminous chemical secrets of a vast garbage dump. Pursue what investigations? Of his soul? As children, Tom and I walked in the rain because we had been forbidden to run. What idea ruled us now? What was our law, and who were our prophets? I could try to emulate a German who found the true gospel of Christ nowhere, except once and irresistibly in "The St. Matthew Passion." Tom, unfortunately, wanted God. Perhaps only mystics pull through. Perhaps Tom's mystical talent, by some mystical definition, was unrecognizable as mystical. If I could trust my intuition, there was not a mystical spark in him. Yet his suffering was real. There are many people in the world who conceive an idea of themselves and must practice it. Was it not remotely possible that if such people set out on a fool's errand, some of them may not after all end on one?

IV

I sat in our unventilated old parlor wondering how to get him to a doctor, or at least drag him to a restaurant if he would dress. Recently his daily fare, I had learned, consisted of three tacos and two Twinkies from a perambulating Mexican in the valley, nothing else. All right, he said, we'd go to The Piggery (a two-hour drive for hamburgers and French fries), but first he wanted to play three recordings for me. "You teach your students to babble in Russian," he said. "What then? What are they going to babble, or isn't that your field? How can you live such an idiotic life! Now sit and listen. I'm throwing you the lifeline."

He produced for my salvation what appeared to be his dearest treasure, the three phonograph recordings which he eventually took with him to Newhall: Nazi marching songs, the album cover showing goose-stepping storm troopers and swastikas; a Red Army chorus;

and a gaggle of gospel singers. So his taste had degenerated to bombast. But why such a muddle of doctrines? Are Fascists, Communists, Christians all God's children?—or was it that they deserved each other?

I said, "Why the Nazis?"

The loudspeaker thundered as he scraped the stylus to make certain that the electrons were flowing properly through the wires. "Did you expect something more modern?" he said, giving me a sarcastic look. "Something innovative, you ass?"

"Something artistic, at least."

"Artistic!" he cried. "By God, I'll make you listen!" Tom liked to share his discoveries, literary, musical, theological, as correctives of error. He could not go through life without making straight the way where he found it crooked. "Shut up now and listen. Listen and think." And putting the three recordings into his antiquated machine, he lay on the dusty couch and closed his eyes.

He had turned the volume on full blast. Evening had come and our darkened parlor filled with the crash of barking Nazis. Coarse and unrelenting, cymbals clashed and a contrabass tuba, *das grosse Bombardon*, drove home the beat like a sledgehammer. Tom's pleasure in the raucous music surprised me. Lying on the couch in that insolent noise, he appeared to drift off into a sweet slumber, as to the sighs of flutes, his face relaxed, faintly smiling.

When he had not stirred for some moments, I retreated softly to the kitchen to make sandwiches, and found the sink full of dirty dishes and garbage. Garbage lay on the floor under the sink, spilled from an overturned paper bag. Cockroaches scattered. Crap on the window sill: a black banana, two rotten tomatoes, a smear of margarine under a rusted knife. In the bread box a loaf of bread bristled with fungus in its unopened cellophane wrapper. In the refrigerator a broken egg had oozed over bacon spotted with mold, beside a filthy skillet with a spatula buried in hard grease. A carton of sour milk, a jar of dill pickles, a small hard sausage called Landjaeger bearing teeth marks, nine cans of sardines, a bowl of yellowish clabber whose chemistry I could not guess, fermenting in its corruption. In the freezer, a carton of popsicles in four flavors, and a cracked bottle of Pepsi Cola. The

Nazis finished singing in the parlor.

From the kitchen doorway I stood looking at him in the silence between the first recording and the second. He had opened his eyes and
lay gazing at the ceiling, studying the darkest plane of the room. The
phonograph clicked. He muttered something, appreciatively, and
closed his eyes again as the Red Army marched in.

He would go to Newhall when he wanted to go, I thought, searching
the kitchen for paper bags to put the garbage in—and stopped, lest I
disturb him. Twenty pounds of junk mail lay on the kitchen table, as
well as some unopened letters, bills. A window-envelope from the Internal Revenue Service appeared to be a tax refund, dated the month
before, also unopened. I returned to my chair in the parlor and sat
through the Red Army and then the gospel singers. Tom seemed
asleep.

When at last the noise ended he pulled himself up and sat heavily
on the couch. Behind him, the sky in the window held the twilight, but
darkness had fully possessed the garden. It was the moment in the day
when you can smell the faint bitterness of eternity. The room itself had
grown dark. I could see Tom's face only in outline, feeling his eyes
upon me. His distant air conveyed an awful solitariness and the question of what to do with it, nudging me into my own isolation. I cast
about for something to divert the threatening uncertainty, the more so
as Tom did not light the lamp and seemed content to sit in the dark.

"You weren't listening," he said.

"Of course I listened. How could I avoid listening?"

"You took your anal compulsions to the kitchen. Fussing."

"Tom, you can't go on like this."

"Like what?"

The spirit sees, the mind argues. Instead of trying to hold the
moment, which might have revealed something rich and strange, I
said what I would have said in the common stir of life: "Living in a
garbage can."

When he spoke again it was in a voice so cold, so hard and alien to
me, that I regretted my visit. "I am not," he said, "living in a garbage
can, you damned fool." And he rose to his feet with weary disgust, as if
by my inattention to his concert I had declined his offer of a priceless
gift.

V

He committed himself to Newhall half a year later, and flying out again I found him comfortably settled in a private room, clean and tidy. The three recordings lay on the floor beside a cheap portable phonograph decorated with red white and blue stripes and the picture of a dancing girl in a bikini.

Apart from the hated medicines that clouded his brain, he liked Newhall well enough and was left in peace to read Carlyle's *Sartor Resartus*, which holds that the Christian church is worn out and must be discarded, like old clothes, but that the underlying religious spirit must be kept alive at all costs.

"Really, you're looking very well," I said.

"You can face anything with stupidity and sound digestion."

Dr. Rogers said he ought to stay in the hospital a while.

Mr. Sladick, whom I then met for the first time, said, "He's marvelous! Absolutely marvelous!"

I had our old house in Los Feliz cleaned, fumigated, and locked.

Tom left Newhall once, in his fourth month there, and went to Los Angeles to seek out Peggy. She had moved as such people do, nobody knew where. In The Piggery he smiled and danced with Sandra at a distance of three feet, aping her gyrations as best he could, jerking his hips and flapping his elbows, from step to step unable to find his center of gravity. Sandra wore dirty jeans with red and yellow patches on the buttocks, and her breath smelled of burnt rubber. She would not dance the slow dances, not liking to be touched, and between beers sat in a telephone booth talking to her sister, she said when she came back, thanking him for the dime. What mattered most to him as a man, Tom said to Sandra, was her personality. If she liked, they could talk at Howard Johnson's? Sandra said, "Fuck off, Buster!"

He said at my third visit, which proved to be the last, "You can't imagine the miles I walked for no reason."

"You must have had something in mind."

"My good passivity."

I could not get him to dress and walk in the hospital's park. He kept to his room, in pajamas. The three recordings lay on his dresser, Nazi, Communist, Christian. Two books lay on his nightstand, C. S. Lewis's *The Problem of Pain* and John Donne's *Biathanatos*, the latter subtitled (I did not trouble to look then) *That Self-homicide is not so naturally Sin that it may never be otherwise.*

He had left Newhall on a Saturday and walked the city till Tuesday morning, for three days and nights, and called Dr. Rogers from a businessmen's convention at The Wilshire East to take him back. At night the demons had come out and the dead rode in cars frothing at the mouth. Worst of all were the Christian churches all day Sunday, truckloads of too-stupid sermons, orthodox and heretical, cesspools of blather.

"And otherwise . . . how are you?" I asked him.

"I'll be going home in a month or two."

"Did Dr. Rogers say so?"

"You don't ask an accountant for an opinion about the soul. We've got to do something about Old Russia. I want to restore the church. Two bastards are waiting to build a restaurant in the graveyard. New thrill. Dine with your loved ones."

The year before, the residents below our hilltop, whose elegant houses of glass and redwood surrounded our acres, had filed a civil suit to deactivate our graveyard, or, as a co-plaintiff demanded, put the graveyard in mothballs. The value of our land having appreciated incredibly over the years, real estate sharks with two-way radios joined the plaintiffs in disputing the sanctity of our burial grounds. An equal contest between piety and greed, enriching the lawyers. In court, counsel for the plaintiff argued that Tom's religious circus made the graveyard an illegal private operation. (His Honor held his head: since when did you object to private operations, and what makes a religion invalid, or valid?) Moreover, although our water was piped in from Lake Tahoe, some neighbors complained that their sinks emitted unwholesome exudations from the stagnant pond in the graveyard, and one matron in black silk pants and silver slippers deposed that on certain nights her kitchen faucets broke out in a cold sweat. Chemical analysis of the water revealed tolerable amounts of putrescence, but the defense showed that the decomposing organic matter came from the gambling casinos in Nevada, or could. Four months after Tom went to Newhall, on the very weekend of his mad walk through Los Angeles, the graveyard was finally closed to fresh corpses, but not ordered removed to a state cemetery.

Tom's debts had piled up. He owed property taxes and court costs, his lawyer had never been paid, shopkeepers and credit companies demanded satisfaction, and the I-Thou Temple in Hollywood, the most imaginative of the gang, had filed a claim against Tom for six years of unpaid dues, printing costs, advertising costs, "service costs," missionary pledges, eighteen percent interest, and consulting fees, all documented. I would have liked to hear some of those consultations, Tom fishing for the spirit in contaminated shallows.

"We have to sell something," I said to Tom.

"Don't sell the church," he said. "You can cut the garden into twenty lots."

Whatever our father's church had been, whatever it might be, Tom felt responsible because its possibilities existed now only in his mind. Perhaps the destruction of the church would let loose upon the air an evil influence to trouble his dreams. He wanted the church restored.

"What will you do with it when it's restored?" I asked.

"Why do anything? I'll sit and look."

"An expensive toy," I said.

"Not a toy. A revelation was always imminent there, even in Father's day."

"It did not happen," I said. "That's why I left."

"It did not happen," he agreed. "But it was always imminent. That's why I stayed."

If he still hoped to experience an idea greater than himself, his expectations had grown smaller. He no longer spoke of the church as an enterprise that might succeed. He merely wanted to restore it as one might a picture.

VI

The day before Tom's funeral I drove up into the mountains of Los Feliz, parked the Hertz car by our old wooden gates, and entered into a silence I had long forgotten. From our desolate avenue of shaggy poplars a bird rose and flapped heavily toward the graveyard, where the trees grew close and dark. Half the vines in the arbor were still putting out leaves, and the latticework trellis, leaning askew, showed streaks of whitewash not yet erased. Passing the priest's house with its carved doors and small square windows designed for Russian winters, I took the path winding through the trees to the church. Here and there tangled bushes and weeds had obliterated the path altogether. At the turn by the dead lemon tree I felt a small stab in my chest, as I saw again the white and the gold of that sad wreck.

Again, as in my childhood, before me rose the large golden onion sprinkled with blue stars, and the smaller asymmetrical domes, one half concealed by the vestry gable, the other near the steps, and the high narrow windows decorated like Christmas cookies and Easter cakes, and the pillars twisted into colorful candy sticks—all teasing me to guess the one thing in life that is real and not an illusion, and saying fairy tales, fairy tales.

Everybody wanted to buy Old Russia, it seemed. Tom had had offers from neighbors, land speculators, transcendental meditators, I-Am-ites, ashramites, nudists, turnip eaters. The faded old church (old for plaster and paint) could easily be rented to some sect or society in search of holy ground in Nixon's Orange County. But by now I had concluded that in a time of God's eclipse nothing so traduces the religious spirit as religious institutions. Believers are unbelievers now, and unbelievers are believers. Between my father's birth in Moscow and my brother's death in Greater Los Angeles, the church had fallen and could continue only as a parody of itself. Rather than letting it revert to a place of worship, whether of God or flowered gurus with pink lips, I would sell the land and see the church bulldozed. Paint blistered and peeling, foliage pressing in upon the windows, tough little bushes splitting the flagstone by the door, the whole sturcture seemed to be sinking into the high grass and nettles. Let the wreckers have it, I thought, and let the builders build, tidy up the grounds and put them to some good use.

But that night in my room at the Sheraton Arms I hesitated still. If not a sentimental scruple, a moral one? The dereliction perhaps of something of value? Would it matter if I returned some day and found the church gone, replaced by Sam's Cuisine, itself fated to crumble? Or found the church restored with hammered gold, a golden cockerel upon the gable, and by the door a tattered beggar dreaming of Byzantium? Church or theater, immortal wreck, what was I to do with it?

Tom would have derided my poetic impulse, pointing out a fallacy in "immortal wreck," *contradictio in adjecto*, which attributes a restorative predicate to a destructive subject. Perhaps in the end he did not care what the place had been, or was, or was to be. *Vocatus atque non vocatus Deus aderit.* Summoned or not summoned God will be there.

What do you do with the imminence of a revelation that does not occur?

VII

I buried him on a sunny Tuesday in Forest Lawn, near the memorial stones of Seventh Day Adventists and a colony of Shintoists. Tom had been so reclusive in his last years that only five people came to the funeral, all strangers to me except Mr. Sladick.

"I wanted to read Tom's motto," he said. "You don't happen to have it?"

"What motto?"

"I don't know it by heart. It's from Carlyle. He kept it with his Nazi record."

I did not engage a preacher to say a few suitable words. Mr. Sladick rode with me to the reception at the Sheraton Arms. A buffet had been set out in the Hawaiian Room. The reception lasted a decent interval, forty minutes.

"A shame to waste such a buffet," said Mr. Sladick. "Look at that canteloupe with sugared fisheyes. If I were you, I'd go into the street and call in the lame and the halt."

Instead we carried gin and tonic and a bucket of ice up to my room. Mr. Sladick was taking the 6:05 Greyhound back to Newhall, time enough to talk about the training of psychiatrists and hospital reforms and the spirit of Napoleon in the work of Léon Bloy. In the jacket of the Nazi recording I found a sheet of typing paper, and unfolded it. Tom had writted with careful calligraphy: "The Universe is not dead and demoniacal, a charnel-house with spectres; but godlike, and my Father's!"

"That's the one," said Mr. Sladick.

I took from the cardboard box the two other recordings, Red Army songs and gospel songs.

"Mr. Sladick," I said, "Tom must have told you something about all these songs. I mean, why did he have such a thing about them?"

"They're all heroic songs. Tom believed in heroes."

Perhaps I had hoped for something better. His explanation irked me and I realized that I would have to make my peace with Tom as best I could. When Mr. Sladick was gone, I plugged in Tom's phonograph and played the three recordings, one after another.

A spirited male choir sang a marching song. *"O, du schöner Westerwald."*

Well, a case could be made: there was something about these songs that went beyond colonels and Gauleiters. Think of Socrates, when he retreated with Laches after the battle of Delium. Think of the flutes piping in his ears when he drank the hemlock. Xanthus heard them in the only memory he brought home with him from the wars, when he recalled that at the storming of Samos, "in the heat of the battle, Pericles smiled on me, and passed on to another detachment."

What can you do with the Red Army Chorus? The Russians marched smartly. They ran, they danced and wailed and dreamed a melancholy tale about somebody's kerchief. They huddled around fires in the bitter snow, ate cats and dogs in Leningrad, killed those same Nazis on the ice of Lake Peipsi, froze to death by the Volga, sitting on their horses. They held the line. And in their last song whole armies of them were returning from Stalingrad, good Bolsheviks all and more coming over the horizon in disordered ranks, carrying red banners and dragging their katyushas, whistling and shouting, having saved Mother Russia for the police state.

But by the time the Christians came on (Burl Ives in gospel songs with a choir of happy believers), I awakened as from a dull sleep to a lucid perplexity. Heads held high and eyes fixed heavenward, smiling through tears at silver linings, Burl Ives and his choir sang and clapped their hands. Could a case also be made for American Protestants, in whose hearts was born the language of automobile insurance policies? In Hartford, Atlanta, and Chicago, see how they rejoice in the imminent destruction of Magog Russia, as promised by God in holy writ. And here are Mormons chased by Presbyterians and Baptists, pulling their covered wagons over the Great Divide and heading for Salt Lake City, where in peace and freedom they can exclude niggers from their priesthood. "Come, come, ye saints."

Yet here too the spirit in their songs soared unperturbed, indifferent to the moralist's certitude and the aesthete's tight nervousness. When all had been disputed and defined, asserted, persecuted, contested, lost, won, vindicated, trivialized, something remained for song to transcend the limits of person, sect, nation, and language itself. To all but the faithful remnant in these last days of scoffers, the usefulness of these Protestant songs had long since been burned away by time and unbelief. These songs were as useless now as the songs the Wehrmacht sang, and the Red Army. Like holy ground, which may not be used for anything, neither for planting nor harvesting, whether of crops or billboards, these songs could at last be called religious. They had become art.

Tom had wanted to serve a Philosopher King, if one could be found among our porkish senators and Texas barracudas. But he scarcely pulled himself through the day and through the night, and for that alone needed metaphysical perspectives, Thomas Carlyle at his elbow. Carlyle gave him a taste of blood and dust, and rattled his brain with the alarm and shock of battle—and it all came to this: the mad primeval discord seeking to be hushed in the hour of spiritual enfranchisement, when the ideal world becomes revealed, God-announcing.

In England, a wise man tells us, where every garden has a brick wall, it is unethical to traffic in abstractions, as the Germans do.

Yet the English, too, have songs.

So I buried my brother and was content to leave him. May it be so. Let him vanish in the Idea, but let its perfection endure.